THE JAMAICAN

SOUL IN DARKNESS

T R CHAMBERS

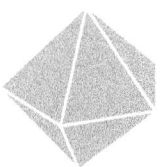

THE JAMAICAN

THE JAMAICAN

SOUL IN DARKNESS

T R CHAMBERS

BOOK 1

OLD MAN TREE PRESS

This book is a work of fiction. Some names, characters, places and incidents are the products of the author's imagination, and are used fictitiously. Resemblance to any actual events, locations, persons, living or dead, is coincidental.

Copyright © 2024 by T. R. CHAMBERS

THE JAMAICAN: SOUL IN DARKNESS

All rights reserved.
Hardcover Laminate Casing

Cover art by Anike Gold of ANIKE GOLD GRAPHIC DESIGN
Cover design by Tanya Chambers of lGSS-P&T LLC
Cover by Tanya Chambers of lGSS-P&T LLC
Editing: Yaya Oluwubarunla

This is the hardcover laminate case edition of THE JAMAICAN: SOUL IN DARKNESS published by Old Man Tree Press. Old Man Tree Press is an imprint of LAZY GAL SWOFIYAH SELF PUBLISHING & THINGS LLC.
PO Box 60392, Rochester, NY 14606

Published and printed in the United States Of America

Old Man Tree Press.
www.oldmantreepress.com

No part of this publication may be reproduced, stored in a retrieval system or transmitted in any form or by any means, electronically, mechanically, photocopying, recording, or otherwise without the prior written consent of the author/Press

Designed by Lazy Gal Swofiyah Self-Publishing & Things LLC

Library of Congress Cataloging-in-Publication Data is available

ISBN 979-8-9916668-6-2
Library of Congress Control Number: 2024949381

Dedication

I dedicate this book to Antonio at the Universales Hotel. Thank you for your generosity. Because of you, I am still alive today.

To my dear friend Preacha who have been the hallmark of my journey, you share a great part of this dedication.

Prologue

Rena watched in sheer horror as the relentless blue water rose ominously, climbing as high as the tallest building on Kensington Avenue in Buffalo. It was a monstrous force, devouring everything in its path as it surged onward with a menacing determination to reach her. Panic surged within her as she started to run, desperate to escape its watery fury, but the faster she tried to run, the slower her legs seemed to move, as if they were weighted down by invisible chains. It became painfully clear to her that she would not be able to outrun its furious advance. Preparing for what felt like certain death, yet refusing to surrender without a fight, she summoned every ounce of strength she had to push her legs into moving a bit faster. Always just one step behind her, the raging water chased her relentlessly, snapping at her heels like a mad bulldog determined to capture its prey.

Her breaths came in rapid succession, each inhale growing more painful as a tightness spread in her chest.

The ferocious, pursuing water dogged her every step all the way across the Mexican border to Laredo

Nuevo, where another vast body of clear blue water awaited her with its menacingly tranquil surface.

"What the hell?" she gasped, taken aback by the impossibility of her situation.

There was a narrow path that lay between the two monstrous bodies of water, each rising steadily to heights that threatened to reach a staggering one hundred and twenty feet, ominously looming on either side. Rena pummeled her feet down the path with all the speed she could muster, desperate to escape before the encroaching waters overcame her entirely.

A flash of Usain Bolt flickered through her mind, igniting a spark of determination. "Usain Bolt! Usain Bolt! Usain Bolt!" she chanted fervently, trying to channel the incredible speed of the world's greatest runner, "Usain Bolt." But in her heart, she knew the unrelenting waters were faster than any man, no matter how legendary.

She was dead now, and the finality of her situation weighed heavily on her. She didn't even have a penny to leave her little cousin, a small contribution to her own burial. How could she die like this, in such an unexpected and tragic manner? "Usain Bolt! Usain Bolt!" She screamed, desperation fueling her voice.

Suddenly, out of nowhere, a bright orange wooden-looking hut materialized, almost like a mirage. It was floating directly towards her amidst the chaos. The high, rough waters had already caught up to her, waves crashing with relentless force. She swam furiously toward the floating orange house, her heart pounding in her chest. Just as the swirling waters began to cover over her, pulling her down toward a watery grave, she felt a strong hand grasp her wrist, pulling her up and out onto the wooden balcony of the small, floating refuge.

Rena rolled onto her side, curling tightly into a ball, coughing up the salty water she had been forced to swallow. Her eyes widened with shock and intensity as her lungs fought for precious air. Her body trembled from both fright and the biting cold, while in her mind she was still fervently chanting: "Usain Bolt! Usain Bolt! Usain Bolt!"

After a few agonizing minutes, when she had somewhat calmed down, she finally looked up at the woman who had so miraculously saved her. The woman was standing over her, cradling a tiny baby girl in her arms, her gaze steady and watchful upon Rena.

"Thank you," she said softly to the woman as she attempted to stand, her body shaky and weak beneath her. Slowly, the relentless coughing that had wracked her body subsided, yet she was still shivering uncontrollably with both cold and fright. Rena followed the silent, familiar-looking woman into the cozy house, feeling a blend of trepidation and relief wash over her. She watched intently as the woman walked over to a small bed and gently laid down the baby girl who had fallen asleep in her arms, her tiny form now at rest.

    Rena found herself looking around the modest yet welcoming dwelling, filled with curiosity and concern, wondering if they were truly going to be safe here, when suddenly, she heard the creaking sound of wood straining against the fierce wind and relentless water outside. The one-room house, though unassuming, was well kept and comfortable. It had a neatly made bed and a small kitchen area complete with a dining table and two chairs that seemed to invite conversation.

    "Are we going to be okay?" she finally mustered the courage to ask the stranger, her voice almost a whisper.

    "This is the safest place for you right now. The house will not sink; it will carry us to where you want to go, but it will not sink," the woman assured her firmly. Yet, Rena noted that the woman did not look particularly happy to have her there, nor did she appear entirely displeased. Rena found herself instinctively moving to the window, gazing out at the endless expanse of water stretching into the horizon. There was not a speck of land in sight. For now, she offered thanks to the gods who were watching over her, feeling a deep sense of gratitude. She was safe.

That very morning, the moment Rena had received the vivid dream, she was still in Buffalo, New York. It was the sign she had been anxiously waiting for before making her next significant move. She could choose to remain if she wanted, but her wanderlust was becoming an overpowering force within her, and the need to escape the erratic and unreliable prick she thought was something—just before her harsh reality check—was an even more compelling urge. The face of Behanzin emerged into her mind's eye, and she found herself imagining the violent act of cutting his head off, a thought that startled her. She immediately shook the troubling image from her mind and redirected her focus back to the dream, seeking clarity and purpose in its fragmented messages.

The dream she had experienced was the pivotal answer she had been anxiously waiting for, the sign she needed to finally make her move. It clearly indicated that while she would inevitably encounter a variety of difficult situations along her journey, she would also be safe, and she absolutely shouldn't allow herself to feel afraid. With that sense of determination and hope, she promptly booked a seat on the Greyhound bus, gathered her already packed belongings filled with memories, and made her way to Mexico City.

The trip had taken a relaxing three days, starting from her Buffalo, New York, all the way to Chihuahua, Mexico; then, she enjoyed another eighteen hours traveling from Chihuahua to Mexico City. She was glad the trip had taken so long, almost four days rent free, sleeping and trying not to worry.

She remembered the moment she crossed into Mexico without going through the immigration process, which had initially concerned her, but the worry did not linger for long. She was liberated from that controlling prick who had always believed he was God's gift to women, and that realization filled her with relief and exhilaration.

During her first week in Mexico, she stayed in a cozy Airbnb located in the vibrant neighborhood of Miguel Hidalgo, Chapultepec. Each day, she stepped out with determination, tirelessly looking for work as an English teacher. Deep down, she knew the search would be challenging, but she had not anticipated just how difficult it would prove to be. At the Airbnb, the owner's mother, with whom she had quickly formed a close friendship, generously provided her with a list of potential places where she could apply for jobs. Meanwhile, the owner's boyfriend, who was employed at an English Teaching Center, suggested she try working for his company, but after learning she lacked the necessary paperwork—which was a vital requirement—he unfortunately backed out of offering her assistance.

Every day, she dressed to impress and diligently followed the helpful tips she had received, yet despite her efforts, nothing substantial came of her applications. Throughout this challenging period, she learned an important lesson: Mexico was markedly different from Asia. In Asia, a place where she had lived for a year before returning to Buffalo, New York, finding jobs as an English teacher was relatively easy; in fact, she would have likely secured a position on her very first day. The geographical proximity to Canada and the United States had allowed for more opportunities and connections. Adding to it all, she had always felt the weight of being from the islands — the Jamaican heritage that made her realize she might not be their first choice in the fierce competition for jobs.

Realizing she had not encountered a single soul who mirrored her appearance, she understood that securing a job in the bustling City was going to be significantly more challenging than she had initially anticipated. However, she was more than ready to face this daunting challenge head-on. It provided her with something to occupy her mind that was far removed from the troubling thoughts of that beast. "Shall I cut off his head for you?" The voice in her head taunted, but Rena chose to ignore the question as she trampled through Mexico City with a determination stronger than ever before, with each step she marched harder than she had anywhere else in her journey. A few curious onlookers watched her, regarding her as if she was someone quite extraordinary and perhaps even a bit strange.

   She arrived in Mexico City completely penniless and utterly alone, hoping to find a job within a day—perhaps two at most. Never in her wildest dreams did she envisage that it would take this long for opportunities to unfold. She found herself at the mercy of fate, surrendering to Jesus.

   On the eighth day of her challenging stay, she finally came across some of the sisters from her church, including Hermanita Rosemaria, who were diligently working out in the field service. Without hesitation, she shared her plight with them, pouring out her heart in hopes of finding some support. They welcomed her warmly, inviting her to attend the church that very night, and just two days later, through their kindness, she was fortunate enough to be provided with a place to stay.

Table Of Content

The Boy In The Room
Matilda's Cry
Curious Things
The Dark Man
The Birds Of The Trees
The Hotel Catalina's Maid
The New Hotel
Go Find A Man
The Twins
A Song To Sun
The Beating Of The Plastic Drum
The Watchers
Hunger Management
The Frying Pan
Meeting Lena
The Dead Body
The Training
Her Monster
A New World
Epilogue

"THE TREES MAY NOT HAVE EYES LIKE US, BUT THEY'RE SEEING EVERYTHING, EVEN THE DUST."

"THE TREES MAY NOT HAVE EARS LIKE US, BUT THEY'RE LISTENING TO EVERYTHING, EVEN WHEN WE FIGHT AND CUSS."

"THE TREES MAY NOT HAVE MOUTH LIKE US, BUT THEY EAT, SPEAK AND NEVER MAKE FUSS."

"THE TREES MAY NOT HAVE FEET LIKE US, BUT THEY'RE WALKING, EVEN WHILE YOU CATCH THE BUS."

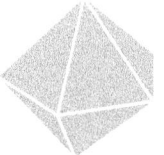

Chapter 1
THE BOY IN THE ROOM

Eight-year-old Tonio sat comfortably in the back seat of the brand new Chevy, gazing out through its tinted dark glasses at the world passing by. His face, despite being covered in dirt from a day of rough play, was as beautiful as the sun and shone just as brilliantly under the warm rays. He was happily licking a dripping strawberry ice cream cone, which, much to his dismay, was causing his tattered and dirty shorts and t-shirt to get stained. His bare, dirty feet bounced up and down with uncontainable joy as he savored the sweet treat. It had been years since he had enjoyed something so delightful. To him, this moment was an unexpected and much-needed treat. Deep down, he felt a swell of gratitude that he had followed his father's seemingly simple instructions.

At first, he had been hesitant; he didn't want to leave his sick father, who was battling the fierce grip of COVID-19. He was also reluctant to leave his younger siblings—his youngest twin brothers and two beloved sisters. As the oldest child, it was his responsibility to take care of them, especially since their father was currently unable to provide that care. Their mother, a dedicated cleaning woman at the hospital, had recently succumbed to the very same disease, leaving Tonio and his siblings to rely on their father, who had tragically caught it while caring for her.

Things had gotten really bad since his father became gravely ill. Though Tonio was doing the very best he could under the circumstances, the daunting task of looking after his younger siblings and his incapacitated father had become an overwhelming, mammoth responsibility for him. Despite the enormous weight on his shoulders, Tonio was not complaining; he understood that this was a temporary phase.

Some days, he would rise early in the morning, embarking on long journeys that often spanned several miles, on foot, to reach the nearest farm where he could lend a hand and earn a meager income. After hours of hard work, he would return home with enough food to sustain them for several days. At times, he would also make his way to the local fruit and vegetable market, scouring the area to glean what the sellers had carelessly discarded. There were even moments when the cupboard was bare, forcing him to sneak into the neighbor's kitchen under the cover of nightfall, just to scrape together their leftovers. They were living in undeniably difficult times that were hard to endure, but as a family, they were all learning to adapt to their harsh reality.

"Tonio," his father moaned one day, struggling through a fit of persistent coughing that lasted nearly two long minutes. "A car is coming tomorrow to pick you up. The driver will take you to my friend, Xavier. He will take good care of you."

"But who's going to take care of you, Papa? And Christos, Tristos, and Rosa, and little Maria?"

"You'll do whatever Xavier tells you to do, and that will help us," his father told him through yet another fit of coughing that rattled his frail body.

If he continued like this, Tonio realized with a heavy heart, he would inevitably end up like Mama, the memory of her haunting his thoughts as he recalled the tragic way she had passed away. She had coughed relentlessly until there was nothing left, ultimately succumbing to the illness. He nodded his head solemnly at his father, his determination growing stronger with each passing moment. Maybe, just maybe, if he worked hard enough, his father could finally get the medicine he desperately needed and avoid the same fate as Mama.

"Okay, Papa. Okay." Tonio did not notice the tears silently rolling down his father's left cheek or the deep shame reflected in his weary eyes. He was far too immersed in envisioning the unyielding work he was about to undertake in order to help support his family.

The following day, when the shiny white Chevy pulled up, looking entirely out of place in front of their run-down wooden shack, he was already packed and mentally prepared to go. After leaving clear instructions with the six-year-old twins, he walked confidently up to the driver who had stepped out of the impressive, brand-new car. The driver, wearing a protective mask, carefully sprayed Tonio with Dettol from a large canister and then squeezed a generous amount of hand sanitizer into the boy's outstretched hands. He watched intently as the boy washed his hands thoroughly, wiping the excess sanitizer onto his dirty, tattered t-shirt, a stark contrast to the cleanliness being enforced. The driver then handed the boy a fresh mask before opening the back door of the vehicle for him. Tonio observed as he put on the mask, then climbed into the car with anticipation. He waved goodbye to his siblings, who had gathered in a line near the car, eyes glued to him, watching his every move. He continued to watch them as they began to chase after the car as it slowly drove off down the street. He didn't look away until they shrank in size, appearing as tiny ants, and eventually disappeared from view. A deep pain welled up in his chest, and silent tears trickled down his cheeks and into his mask.

He was a man now, embarking on a journey to work diligently to take care of them. Consoled by that empowering thought, he felt himself cheer up. He looked around his small, unfamiliar surroundings with his beautifully large, purple eyes filled with wonder. He had never had the opportunity to ride in anything so luxurious or fancy before. Taking a deep breath, he inhaled deeply. The rich scent of new leather permeated through his mask, filling his nostrils, and made the unknown feel almost tangible and real. He imagined this specific aroma to be the smell of the elegant car he would one day drive when he finally reached the age of eighteen. As his curiosity peaked, he began to touch everything within reach that his hands could grab hold of, committing each sensation and detail to memory, creating a cherished connection with this moment.

"Put your seat belt on," the driver ordered firmly, his tone leaving no room for argument. The boy quickly obeyed, fastening the strap across his lap. Thirty minutes later, Tonio thought they had finally reached their long-awaited destination when the driver unexpectedly stopped in front of a colorful ice-cream shop. But unfortunately, he had only paused to chat with a friend he spotted outside. After what felt like an eternity of waiting, ten minutes later he returned with a delicious ice-cream cone, handing it to the boy with a smile.

Tonio eagerly finished his cone, savoring every bite, and then began focusing intently on the road ahead. He wanted to see where they were heading, just in case he needed to figure out a way to walk back home by himself. However, he was too tired and comfortable after the exhausting journey and soon fell asleep, succumbing to the warmth of the car and the gentle motion.

Six hours later, he felt the driver gently shaking him awake. To his surprise, they had finally reached their destination. Tonio clambered out of the vehicle and stretched his limbs, looking around with wide eyes brimming with curiosity and a multitude of questions. "Is this really where I'm going to work?" he asked, staring at the impressive hotel lobby entryway—a mere couple feet away from the parking lot, which was enclosed with weathered white painted zinc fences. He noticed that the paint was peeling in places, and the grounds needed some serious repairing. The foliage that lined each side of the entryway to the parking lot was tall but oddly sparse, adding to the air of neglect surrounding the location.

The little boy wandered, deep in thought, about the kind of work he might possibly do here in this bustling place. Maybe they would assign him to the kitchen, which he believed would be the best spot to be in. He imagined all the delicious food he would prepare and send to his brothers and sisters, feeling a rush of excitement and growing impatient to get on with it.

"Xavier is here?" The driver asked the receptionist, who was standing behind a high glass wall, her demeanor professional yet warm.

"No, but you can leave the boy here," she replied, her voice calm and steady.

Standing in the brightly colored orange reception area was Sao, the hotel plumber, whose presence was as dependable as his profession suggested. He held out his hand to the little boy, beckoning him forward with a friendly smile. Tonio looked uncertainly at the driver, seeking reassurance. The driver nodded his head encouragingly, and thus, the little boy took Sao's outstretched hand and began to follow him up the stairs to the second floor, arriving at Room 2017A. "Take off your clothes and get into the shower," Sao instructed the little boy firmly but kindly before exiting the room.

Having caught a glimpse of his reflection in the mirror, Tonio quickly realized he was far too dirty for the kitchen and hurriedly followed Sao's instructions without hesitation. Sao returned just minutes later, bringing with him clean clothes that were perfectly sized for the boy, along with a fresh washcloth. Although there were large towels in the bathroom, he noticed the absence of a washcloth, making him feel even more grateful for the one Sao provided.

Sao squeezed a generous amount of soothing shampoo shower gel onto the plush washcloth and began to scrub Tonio thoroughly from head to toe.

"I've already bathed," Tonio complained petulantly. "I just finished washing my entire body."

It felt like an injustice to him, a slight that he couldn't quite ignore. After all, he was a man, or at least he considered himself one, and he seethed quietly at the indignity of his current situation. He had been bathing himself ever since he turned four years old and had maintained a pretty good record of cleanliness, if he did say so himself. However, he chose to keep his mouth shut while the unfamiliar stranger continued scrubbing him vigorously in the hot water, ensuring that every part of him was properly cleaned. When the time came to dry off, Sao reached for one of the two large white towels adorned with bright red lettering that the boy couldn't decipher. He had never learned to read, a skill that had always eluded him.

"What's the name of this place?" he asked Sao, the large man, feeling curious yet hesitant.

"What! You cannot read?" Sao exclaimed, vigorously drying the boy's back and buttocks as if it was the most surprising revelation.

"No, I was supposed to go to school, but Mama got sick," Tonio replied, his voice tinged with a mix of sadness and frustration.

There was no response from Sao; he was too engrossed in making sure that every conceivable crack and crevice of the boy was clean and free of dirt. When he finally noticed that there was no sign of dirt remaining on the pristine white towel, he felt a sense of satisfaction wash over him. Sao then dressed the boy neatly, giving him a firm instruction to sit on the bed.

"Don't move; I'll be right back," he ordered, leaving Tonio in a state of bewilderment and curiosity.

Tonio sat quietly on the bed, obediently, his eyes fixed on the man as he exited the room. He looked around the medium-sized room, taking in the pale green wallpaper that adorned the walls and the imposing king bed—the largest Tonio had ever encountered. Back at home, he slept on the hard floor alongside his four siblings, while his Mama and Papa shared a small, cramped bed in the corner of their modest living space. But now that his beloved Mama was no longer with them, his Papa had sternly ordered them not to climb onto the bed, fearing they might catch something unpleasant. As the thought of his parents washed over him, a tear rolled down Tonio's cherry pink, clean cheeks, glistening in the soft light at the thought of their absence. He was a man now, after all. He should muster the strength to man-up. Wiping at the tear in frustration, he waited impatiently for the man to return, eager for his guidance to the kitchen where he would begin his new responsibilities.

The Jamaican

Chapter 2
MATILDA'S CRY

R ena finally set the heavy knapsack down on the plush, carpeted floor, right in front of her room door, letting out a breath of relief that filled her with a mix of exhaustion and gratitude. She had trudged along with it weighing down her back for a grueling thirty minutes, and now her shoulder blades were practically screaming in protest while her spine grumbled in discomfort. But despite the discomfort, she welcomed the pain with a determined smile and now sent it off, releasing it with a heavy sigh.

She felt an overwhelming sense of fatigue and disgruntlement wash over her. The shopping trip had been far more costly than she had anticipated, as she had spent twice as much at the supermarket for the same amount of goods she typically purchased. This was the second time she found herself shelling out over four hundred pesos for basic items that had previously cost her less than two hundred and fifty pesos at her go-to supermarket. The impact of the pandemic on prices was becoming increasingly burdensome, and she couldn't help but wonder how she was ever going to navigate through these challenging times and survive.

As she stood there, she tried to push aside the haunting images of the many homeless individuals she had encountered on the streets during her return to the hotel. In her heart, she understood she was homeless too; however, the manager had shown her kindness and taken pity on her, allowing her to stay in the modest room. Perhaps, if fortune smiled upon her, she might manage to scrape together enough funds to pay him back by the time she was ready to leave.

In this moment of reflection, she found a sliver of comfort and sent a silent "thank you" to her friend, Kimmy, who lived in Rochester, New York. Kimmy had generously sent her twenty-five American dollars, of which five was intended to offset the negative balance in her bank account, while the remaining twenty was meant for her to nurse carefully. To her dismay, that small amount was now depleted, leaving her with no ability to even buy the essential water she needed. She pondered anxiously, how was she going to cook her meals without proper water? Using the water from the bathroom sink was certainly out of the question; it had completely failed the tea test, and she couldn't bear the thought of using it to cook her food.

She was thinking far too much for her own good. With a determined breath, she sent all distracting thoughts scattering from her mind as she opened the door to her temporary quarters. The room inside was expansive, featuring a comfortable queen-sized bed with two side tables firmly attached to the wall on either side. The four walls were enveloped by a very busy and vibrant orange abstract-designed wallpaper that seemed to pulse with energy. The window coverings and bedspread shared the same vivid orange hues, adorned with geometric patterns that elegantly complemented the chaotic beauty of the wallpaper. The plush carpeted flooring, rich in darker tones, anchored the lively atmosphere of the room. Although the sizable window in the room did not open, a ceiling fan circulated clean, refreshing air, assisted by a smaller window located in the bathroom.

    The bathroom, which was only about half the size of the spacious bedroom, boasted ceramic tiles that stretched from ceiling to floor, with a dazzling array of colors that danced before the eyes, depending on where one looked. The small window served both the bathroom and the bedroom, ensuring both spaces received the necessary quality air.

    Rena dragged her knapsack wearily into the room and carefully closed the door behind her. Establishing a sense of security, she stuffed the t-shirt she had designated for that purpose into the gap beneath the door to block any escaping light. Once she was satisfied that no light could leak out, she further secured the door by placing her two heavy suitcases, which had accompanied her on countless journeys over the years, against it. This was her form of a nomad's protection. For that's exactly how she defined herself—a nomad, always on the move and seeking new experiences.

Leaving her bag of groceries nestled alongside the suitcases, she walked the few steps to the large window, hoping to catch a glimpse of her friends outside. Nuck had his big, expressive eyes opened wide immediately, beaming a huge smile at her. It took a few deliberate seconds for Tuck to finally situate his gaze in her direction. He was looking thoughtfully at the cloudless blue sky, clearly filled with some concerns that tugged at his heart. This subtle shift let her know there might be a chance of rain later in the day. When he finally turned and looked at her, he winked his right eye mischievously, a playful glint in his gaze. She couldn't help but laugh at their antics. They both were grinning wickedly at her, matching expressions of joy illuminating their faces. Her heart sang with delight at the spontaneous moment.

For a brief moment, the weariness she had been feeling earlier simply vanished into thin air. She took a deep, refreshing breath, happy that she had stumbled upon these delightful friends. She gave them another warm smile before leaving them behind to go wash the dust off her body, eager to feel refreshed before unpacking her groceries.

What was she going to cook without water? Rena questioned herself as she finished applying lotion to her skin, trying to shake off the nagging feeling of uncertainty. All the fresh vegetables she had purchased needed thorough washing before she could even think about cooking them. She quickly dressed in the small confines of the bathroom, the sound of her own movements echoing slightly around her, before proceeding to her little food storage area where she began to unpack her recent purchase. Taking out the last item from her knapsack, she revealed a litre of Alimento Liquid De Coco, a rich coconut milk made from freshly grated coconut. She had vivid memories of the last two brands she had tried, both of which had been such disappointments, and she fervently hoped this one would prove to be different.

The mere thought of going downstairs to ask for some water was not a welcoming one, so she quickly shook it from her mind. She reasoned that when she was truly desperate, she might have to swallow her pride and go down there to bother them for help. For the moment, however, she would settle for the cup of water she had left in a bottle she had received from one of the hotel maids. The creamy coconut milk would hopefully supplement the water just enough. Rena pondered over a simple yet satisfying meal she could whip up using the two key ingredients.

She was becoming increasingly impatient with herself for still debating what to prepare for dinner, as her stomach growled in protest. It was hard to ignore the fact that she had not eaten anything at all in nearly three days—a now frequent occurrence that she was not proud of. Taking a banana from the counter, she quickly peeled it and forced half of it into her mouth, savoring the sweet flavor as she closed her eyes and moaned in pleasure at the modest treat. Suddenly, the persistent crying of the female cat, Matilda, reached her ears, snapping her back to reality, and she instantly came to attention. Was it a warning of some sort? Or was the cat merely hungry? Rena listened intently for any further sounds, but only heard the grumbling of her own stomach in response.

The black cat was thoroughly peeved that her master had given away yet another one of her precious kittens.

"Sorry, Matilda, you were going to leave them after a couple of weeks, anyway," Rena mentioned nonchalantly, seeing the feline in her mind's eyes.

Matilda didn't answer, her piercing gaze spoke volumes. Rena had been channelling the cat since they first brought her to the hotel just a couple of months ago. The cat was specifically supposed to warn her whenever there was a child brought onto the premises for unnatural purposes. But lately, since the cat had given birth to her kittens, she had become increasingly quiet—until now.

Rena went back to eating her ripe banana while pouring some of the creamy coconut milk into a cup to wash the sweet fruit down. She was trying her best to use the milk sparingly, but thirst ultimately got the better of her, prompting her to pour another generous half a cup and chug it down eagerly. Suddenly, the piercing scream of a small boy, echoing nearby, shattered the unusual quiet that had enveloped the hotel. Rena's heart skipped a beat in response to the distressful sound.

"This is your first time, I know, but you have to get used to it. It won't hurt so badly next time," she heard a man saying gently in Spanish. But unfortunately, the boy wasn't listening; instead, he was screaming bloody murder. Panic washed over Rena as she ran to the window and looked anxiously at her friends.

"Please help him. Please!" she pleaded silently to them, her eyes wide with concern. But Nuck just smiled hugely at her, blinking in a relaxed manner, while Tuck was gazing up at the sky, looking rather preoccupied. Although there were no clouds in sight, the wind was picking up speed. He was obviously worried about the occupants they were currently boarding.

"Please help the boy, please," Rena begged once more, her large, glistening tears rolling down her cheeks uncontrollably as she felt the weight of despair pressing down on her heart. She felt utterly powerless in this moment, receiving no response whatsoever to her heartfelt pleas.

"Great Mother, please help him," Rena whispered desperately as she turned her attention to SOURCE, clinging tightly to the hope of a miracle that could turn the situation around. She reluctantly left the window where she had silently watched and returned to the door, her ears straining to catch any sound. The boy's cry was muffled, and she imagined the man's hand pressed over his mouth, attempting to quiet his desperate cries.

"Great Mother SOURCE, please help him," Rena cried out into the vast space within her mind, hoping earnestly to summon a response, picturing someone heroic going to the boy's rescue. Relief washed over her momentarily when she sensed a shift in the boy's energy; it had quieted, as if he felt a glimmer of hope.

"Thank you," she murmured to the immense void in her mind, filled with gratitude.

Rena then moved to sit on the large ottoman, which was the only piece of seating arrangement available in the room. With her legs carefully folded beneath her and her back held straight, she closed her eyes and allowed her very essence to transcend the physical confines of her body.

As her spirit ventured forth, it walked effortlessly through the walls and out into the dimly lit corridor where the scream had originated. Matilda, perched gracefully in front of Room 2017A, lifted her head and looked up at the ethereal being, her curiosity piqued. With a soft meow, she watched intently as the being glided through the closed door, entering the room where the boy was in need of urgent help.

    There was a woman, whose form was completely unrecognizable, already lingering in the dimly lit room. She was tenderly snuggling a beautifully innocent little boy with striking, shocking purple eyes, around eight years of age, beneath her flickering right arm. Their gazes were intensely focused on the two large, naked men kneeling helplessly on the bed. The men's penises were grotesquely being taken over by a crawling mass of maggots. Rena felt a deep sense of shock to see the maggots slowly, mercilessly eating away at their manhood, dismantling whatever dignity remained. Their mouths were tightly sealed shut, rendering them utterly voiceless. They seemed to be rendered motionless by invisible hands that gripped them firmly. Only the frantic movements of their eyes betrayed the sheer fear and pain they were experiencing.

    The flickering woman, however, did not appear to be in any hurry as she calmly observed the maggots working their sinister magic over the two unfortunate men. It was exactly the horrific scene Rena had imagined when she had first stumbled upon the grim revelation that child prostitution was being brazenly conducted within this hotel. One of the men suddenly looked at the boy with eyes stricken by pain, pleading for understanding.

The Jamaican

"Do you know him?" The flickering woman asked with a hint of surprise mingled with curiosity.

"Yes, he owns the farm I sometimes worked," the boy replied, displaying a level of maturity and insight startling for someone his age.

"Oh, so this was his plan, then," she reflected, recognizing the heavy weight of worry and concern the boy held for his family. She contemplated the dying father who had sent his son forth into this dreadful circumstance, fully aware of the peril that awaited him. Images of the sprawling acres of farmland, laden with the many beautiful houses the farmer had built, flooded her mind, and she made a decisive resolution.

The maggots had gruesomely eaten away the men's penises and were now lethally working their way up to their scrotums. She cast a searching glance at the farmer for a moment, then coldly stated, "The boy's father will meet his demise within a couple of hours, but I suppose you already knew that when you cunningly ensured his mother contracted the virus, fully aware that the father would inevitably suffer the same fate."

The farmer's surprise was painfully evident, creating a stark contrast to his agony.

"You, however, are now tasked with taking all five children and arranging for them to be housed comfortably in one of your many beautiful residences. You will nurture and care for them as if they were your own flesh and blood. Each child must have a room of their own, and they should be enrolled in school by the end of the week at the latest. It is imperative that they receive three nutritious meals a day, and that you employ a nanny to attend to their various personal needs. In addition, they should be provided with beautiful clothing to wear. And should you dare to look at any one of them with a hint of dubious sexual intent, the maggots I am leaving lodged in your body will multiply exponentially and ensure your demise. If you dare mistreat them in any way, the maggots will swiftly finish you off. If you force them into manual labor—unless they willingly choose to help—the maggots will finish you off without mercy. And don't even think about attempting to rid yourself of them; nothing you do will have any effect. Be certain to hire a proper nanny who will assist in tending to their emotional and psychological well-being, ensuring they feel safe and loved. So help me, the maggots will multiply and finish you off, from the inside."

    She looked down at the beautiful little boy before her, tenderly patting his small head, which was covered with soft, raven black hair that glistened in the dim light.

    "He's going to take you and your siblings to his farm, a lovely place where you will find happiness. You will have a house there, with each of you having your very own cozy room to call your own. You're going to see that your brothers and sisters are well taken care of, okay?"

"What about Papa?" the boy asked, his voice filled with innocent concern.

"He's too sick, my dear; he'll not make it."

She didn't need to tell the boy that his father's wickedness had ultimately sent him to his tragic end. If he had just kept his son near, he could have recovered and properly seen to their well-being. The father had chosen the wrong path, and now, he would pay dearly for it.

Both scrotums had now been eaten away completely, leaving a grotesque reminder of their former selves. The woman turned her gaze to the other man, whose inward parts were already under siege by a writhing mass of maggots.

"I will release you now," she intoned with an unsettling calmness. "Drive straight home. You must go to your backyard, the grim resting place of all eighteen children you buried in silence. The maggots lurking within you will finish you off there, no doubt about that. And if you dare step just one toe off track, they will ensure you experience the worst possible agony you could ever conceive—right up to the very end. Your sole responsibility now is to take care of those children waiting for you on the other side. So don't hesitate or delay."

Within mere seconds after finishing her chilling discourse, she had both men and the boy, still snugly tucked under her arm, dressed and appearing ready to depart. The boy's previously distressed anus had been expertly repaired, with all traces of blood miraculously vanished. She had deftly wiped all memory of the traumatic event from his innocent mind, shielding him from the horrors that had just transpired.

Although the farmer's hairless, crotchless groin area had healed surprisingly well, he could still feel the wriggling maggots gradually moving around inside his body—a sinister warning from the flickering woman.

The farmer reached out, grasping the boy's small hand, and together the two departed the room, leaving behind the sinister atmosphere. The other man, the unfortunate hotel plumber, was not so lucky. Pain gnawed at him, evident in the way he walked slowly, with each step punctuated by excruciating agony. His body trailed a foul, pungent smell of human decay that lingered in the air, a haunting reminder of the horrors he was now forced to confront.

~~~~~~~~~

The woman looked at Rena's being with familiar, knowing eyes that spoke volumes. "Sarai said hi," she said, winking playfully, then she vanished from the room as if she were a whisper of smoke. Within mere seconds, Rena's ethereal being returned to its vessel,

The Jamaican

bringing a sense of clarity. She quickly got up from the ottoman and hurried to the window, her heart racing with a mix of excitement and nostalgia. Her gaze landed on Sarai, the very first one to open her eyes for Rena to see, so many months ago when everything began to change.

Sarai's eyes were as wide as tea cups, filled with warmth and light, and her smile was even bigger than Rena had remembered. Tears of profound gratitude began to run down Rena's cheeks as she felt an overwhelming sense of love.

"*Thank you so much,*" she said to them, broadcasting the message on the frequency they had cultivated for their unique form of communication.

"*You're welcome.*" Sarai winked back at her, a playful gesture that was as reassuring as it was sweet, and then started moving gracefully in the breeze. The others followed suit in a delicate dance with the wind. Soon, all traces of their smiling faces were gone, leaving behind nothing but normal trees bending and swaying gently in the light gusts of the wind.

"THE TREES MAY NOT HAVE EYES LIKE US, BUT THEY'RE SEEING EVERYTHING, EVEN THE DUST."

"THE TREES MAY NOT HAVE EARS LIKE US, BUT THEY'RE LISTENING TO EVERYTHING, EVEN WHEN WE FIGHT AND CUSS"

"THE TREES MAY NOT HAVE MOUTH LIKE US, BUT THEY EAT, SPEAK AND NEVER MAKE FUSS."

"THE TREES MAY NOT HAVE FEET LIKE US, BUT THEY'RE WALKING, EVEN WHILE YOU CATCH THE BUS."

Chapter 3
CURIOUS THINGS

It was with much relief and happiness that Rena joyfully moved away from the window to sort out her newly purchased bounty from the supermarket. She was genuinely delighted that things turned out exactly the way they did. She didn't always have the good fortune to witness the end result of her heartfelt prayers. In fact, she could hardly remember a time when her prayers had manifested in such a wonderful way.

However, her happiness was fleeting as her vessel unceremoniously reminded her of its pressing need. Her hunger returned with a vengeance, and she couldn't help but feel impatience for dinner to be cooked. She returned to her food storage, her mind preoccupied with possibilities. She really didn't know what she wanted to cook just yet, and as she pondered, she picked up the only knife she owned along with one of the three ripe oranges she had just purchased. Without hesitation, she swiftly peeled the orange. Her toes curled with delight as her tongue acknowledged the burst of sweetness. She had not tasted one this sweet in quite a little while. Tempted to peel another, she had to sternly remind herself that there were indeed other days to come for indulging.

Remembering the succulent mango she had selected, she eagerly went back to the box where she kept all her perishable items. With a sense of determination, she ransacked the box until she finally unearthed the mango nestled within the large plastic bag—an intentional choice she had made for keeping the mango alongside her other fruits and veggies. She knew she would need them soon for her trash.

After washing the mango carefully in the bathroom sink and drying it thoroughly with her soft towel, she took an enormous, satisfying bite. Her toes curled involuntarily at the burst of flavor. The mango was incredibly sweet, delightfully sweet, in fact. It was the sweetest she had tasted since moving to the vibrant streets of Mexico City over eight months ago. With her eyes closed, she reveled in the exquisite taste that danced upon her tongue. Like a starving child, she eagerly sucked the mango seed clean, savoring every last bit of juice. When there was nothing left but the pit, she reluctantly threw the seed in the garbage, a small pang of regret settling in her stomach. Still ravenous, she returned to the box, searching to see what else she could glean from her meager supplies.

Rena absolutely hated going hungry for such a long stretch; nothing she had eaten satisfied her cravings. During her trip to the supermarket, she hadn't bought much fruit—just three bananas, three oranges, two crisp apples, a single juicy mango, and a few under-ripe guavas. The guavas were hardly ripe, unfortunately not soft enough for her liking. She knew these fruits wouldn't last very long, but she sincerely hoped she could be disciplined enough to make them last.

As she continued to rummage through her snacks, the pack of Oreo cookies caught her eye—the only junk food she had allowed herself to squeeze onto the shopping list. The bag was already open, and before she could even stop herself, one of the sweet, chocolate sandwich cookies was quickly in her mouth. She downed four more absentmindedly, closing the bag afterward to save the rest for later. Yet, she was still hungry. Finally, after some deliberation, she settled on oatmeal porridge for dinner. That should fill the growing gap in her stomach, or so she hoped.

The orange one-burner electric stove, which a thoughtful church sister had graciously purchased for her some months ago, was now sitting prominently on one of the side tables, almost directly in front of the sunlit large window. Her friends, who had momentarily forgotten that they were play-acting as if they were blowing dramatically in the wind, stood motionlessly, transfixed and watching her with great intensity. Rena had long learned during the trying times of quarantine lockdown that the roles had fundamentally reversed. She had become the caged human attraction in a zoo—a fish in a bowl was probably a more fitting and humorous description—and they were now the curious onlookers peering in. She could feel their eyes glued to her, observing everything she did with a keen interest. Meanwhile, she had grown accustomed to watching them remain unmoving while the other trees danced furiously around them in the wind, seemingly enjoying their robust freedom.

 Rena offered them a confident smile through the glass, cheerfully going about her simple culinary task. She poured a cup of coconut milk into one of the two charming blue pots she had been guilted into accepting from the aforementioned Mexican church sister. Rena couldn't help but chuckle as she recalled the comical scene in the supermarket when Hermanita Rosemaria had cried serious crocodile tears upon hearing her insistence that it was too much and that she simply couldn't accept such a generous gift.

"Rena, I buy you gift, you need. Take," Hermanita Rosemaria had firmly insisted in her endearing broken English.

"No, Hermanita, mucho, mucho claro. I cannot accept them; they're far too expensive," she replied in a lighthearted manner, laughter bubbling up between her words. She had merely pointed out how cute the pots were, thinking they would make a delightful decoration, not expecting her to go ahead and purchase them. But Hermanita Rosemaria had cheerfully made up her mind to be generous in her gift-giving.

"No, you need, you take." When Hermanita saw that the younger woman was playing stubborn and refusing to accept the gifts, she immediately turned on the water works, effectively shocking and guilting Rena into finally conceding to her older sister's generosity. At that particular moment, they were at a different Soriana Supermarket located in Miguel Hidalgo, conveniently near the beautiful Chapultepec Park. Rena vividly recalled how she had quickly glanced around the bustling supermarket, making sure that no one was observing their interaction. She didn't want anyone to misinterpret the situation and think she was hurting the older woman in any way.

"Okay, okay Sister, please stop crying. I will take your gift," Rena finally told her, wrapping a reassuring hand around the woman's shoulders in a gesture of consolation.

Hermanita Rosemaria was known for being a shameless cryer, and in that moment, Rena realized she had been had.

Chuckling softly with residual guilt, and feeling grateful that her sister had insisted on giving the gifts, Rena carefully placed the blue pot on the orange one-burner stove, all the while pretending to be oblivious to the curious stares of her friends peering through the nearby window.

~~~~~~~~~

Rena was incredibly happy that she was able to help the sister just a couple of days later—in a way that was both supportive and inconspicuous. They were out in the field service when Rena noticed that Hermanita Rosemaria was making frequent trips to the bathroom, which caught her attention. The sister was visibly complaining about the pain she was experiencing in her lower back. After observing the last three trips to the bathroom in a remarkably short span of just fifteen minutes, Rena turned to the sister and said, "Let me show you a stretch that's particularly good for alleviating your lower back pain."

With her field service bag resting on the ground beside her, Rena positioned herself facing the towering concrete wall fence that lined the road they were walking on. She raised herself on the tips of her toes, ensuring her back was straight, and extended her hands up high above her head as if reaching for the clouds. "Do you see what I'm doing?" She asked the sister. "My legs are straight, my spine is straight, my head is tilted back, my face is looking up toward the beautiful sky, and my hands are fully extended straight above me. Do you think you can give that a try?"

"Yes," the sister had replied with enthusiasm.

Eager to give it a try herself, she placed her bag next to Rena's on the ground and carefully went up on her tippy toes. While she was engrossed and busy focusing on mirroring Rena's action, Rena gently held onto the sister's left shoulder with her left hand, while her right hand expertly walked her fingers down the church sister's spine, all the way to her tailbone. So deeply concentrated on the task at hand was Hermanita Rosemaria that she didn't notice Rena's fingers applying a slightly increased pressure, as they left her tailbone and made their way back up her spine, reaching up toward her neck.

When Rena had seen to it that the bones were correctly placed, she moved to the sister's right side and gently held on to her upper back, still using her left hand while resting her right hand on Hermanita's chest.

"Remember, you have to try to keep your back straight, and your chest pushed out, head held high, and your eyes looking directly into the sky. Keep your hands firmly on the wall," she said firmly when she noticed Hermanita Rosemaria was about to let go. The older woman quickly returned her extended hands to the wall with labored breath, not even noticing Rena was performing Reiki on her, from her chest to her belly button, seamlessly replacing the new energy where her own had sadly diminished. Once she was finished, Rena placed her hands firmly on the sister's belly and ordered with authority.

"Keep your back straight." Hermanita Rosemaria forced her noticeably hunched back straighter, her breath coming in short gasps as if she were running a marathon.

"Okay, you can relax now," Rena instructed, finishing with her careful administration. The sister relaxed with immense relief, leaning against the wall, grateful for the support.

"You think you can do this exercise two to three times a day every day?" She asked the exhausted woman.

"Yes, I do it," the woman responded, her voice filled with excitement. Rena laughed, "Good, you must do it exactly like how you just did it. It will keep your bones aligned and your back straight."

Hermanita Rosamaria's slight hunch was not fixed immediately. It would have been questionable if she had fixed the woman's hunch so quickly.

"Yes, I do it," she repeated, her voice brimming with enthusiasm.

Rena remembered the older sister coming back to her a couple of days later, complaining about the disappearance of the pain in her back and her less frequent trips to the bathroom. But now there's a new pain. She sounded accusatory, as if she missed her frequent visits to the bathroom and the pain in her back. The older sister was blaming it on the exercise, not noticing the notable change in her physical appearance. Her neck was a couple of centimeters longer, the hunch was less pronounced, and she looked a little taller.

"Maybe you should go to the doctor to see that everything is okay," Rena suggested, concerned for the woman's well-being.

The sister was so incredibly miffed by the ongoing absentee ailments and the new one that had just cropped up, she couldn't help but start complaining loudly to all the members in the group who were out in the field that day. She had developed a reputation as a huge gossip, and Rena stood out as the strange newcomer in their midst. A peculiar sister, whose vibrant color, distinct appearance, and unique culture were starkly different from those around her. When Hermanita Rosemaria finally finished her long-winded complaints, she had fat, heavy tears rolling down her cheeks like molten rivers. They all turned to look at Rena with deep distrust and lingering suspicion in their eyes. At that moment, Rena made a quiet promise to herself to be more careful and mindful in the future. A couple of weeks later, the church sister with whom she was currently lodging made the difficult decision to kick her out.

"We don't understand you. The neighbors don't trust you, and they don't like you," Sister Kenya's mother had conveyed, through the English interpreter, Pedro, who happened to be her son-in-law and a French church brother. Less than a month later, the unexpected pandemic hit, sending the entire Western world into a chaotic frenzy and leaving Rena jobless just three weeks after starting her new job in Mexico City.

The oats porridge cooked down in rich, creamy coconut milk and sweetened generously with Nestle Condensed Milk was simply mouthwatering and inviting. Rena unplugged the stove—it didn't have an adjustable knob, so she found herself unable to turn it down, which felt a bit inconvenient. She didn't eat the delicious porridge immediately, as she had initially wanted to. Instead, savoring her meal while she was safely tucked in bed felt like a much more favorable option. Already dressed comfortably in her cozy house clothes, she just needed to take a moment to make her bed to create a welcoming space. She stripped the bedspread, blankets, and sheets from the hotel bed she had meticulously made before heading out to the supermarket earlier that day. Carefully folding them the way she usually did, she spread them out on the floor in the bathroom. The thickest blanket was spread out on the hard floor, providing a safeguard against the biting cold. On top of that, she placed the sheets carefully. The smaller, thick blanket was set neatly in the middle of another sheet, contributing to her comfort. The thin, king-sized white sheet she had purchased at Walmart in Buffalo was used not only for warmth but primarily for protection from the hotel bedspreads.

The small cutting board—a thoughtful gift from Seti, her dear friend from Buffalo—was thoughtfully positioned on the floor, serving as a makeshift side table. Rena placed her porridge pot atop it, along with her small, half filled, water bottle. The pillows, plush and inviting, were set against the bathroom wall in a comfortable position to support her back.

On her way back into the room, she noticed her friends were still watching her, intently, unmoving in the soft breeze while the other trees were being blown hither and tither, their leaves rustling gently in the wind. Nuck and Tuck's eyes were still wide with curiosity, wearing their bright, infectious smiles that radiated warmth. Rena couldn't help but laugh at them, their enthusiasm contagious. She then went about the task of remaking the hotel bed, using only the top spread to ensure that it looked tidy. If anyone should happen to come into the room, they would certainly think the bed was properly made and orderly. Her bag, containing all her personal papers, notes, and other essentials, was sprawled out on the floor, in the bathroom.

The plastic basin she had been traveling around with in Mexico City, intended for washing her clothes and hair, was currently turned upside down, serving as an impromptu table for her laptop. The toilet seat was covered over with one of the large white towels provided by the hotel, adding a touch of comfort to the otherwise basic setup.

Now that everything was neatly in place, she felt a wave of impatience wash over her as she eagerly anticipated diving into her porridge. She grabbed the rest of the uneaten Oreos, a delightful treat, and waved to her friends on her way back to the bathroom.

"*See you later*," she communicated silently to them on the frequency they often conversed, a shared understanding passing between them. She turned on the lights in the bathroom, the bright illumination contrasting with the dimness outside, and closed the door behind her. After finding her favorite spot on the floor, she settled in and turned on her phone to Youtube, ready to unwind.

The porridge was sweet and hot, perfectly comforting, and the addition of coconut milk did not disappoint; it added strength, richness, and delightful flavor to every single bite. It was so much better than the others she had tried before; honestly, it was the best yet. Soon, the porridge was finished, but still feeling somewhat unsatisfied, she found herself tempted to go make some more. But she reminded herself that tomorrow was another day, and with that thought, she pushed aside the craving and savored the moment.

"THE TREES MAY NOT HAVE EYES LIKE US, BUT THEY'RE SEEING EVERYTHING, EVEN THE DUST."

"THE TREES MAY NOT HAVE EARS LIKE US, BUT THEY'RE LISTENING TO EVERYTHING, EVEN WHEN WE FIGHT AND CUSS."

"THE TREES MAY NOT HAVE MOUTH LIKE US, BUT THEY EAT, SPEAK AND NEVER MAKE FUSS."

"THE TREES MAY NOT HAVE FEET LIKE US, BUT THEY'RE WALKING, EVEN WHILE YOU CATCH THE BUS."

Chapter 4
THE DARK MAN

It was still early evening, but the walk to the supermarket she had taken earlier—on a notably hungry belly—had truly taken a toll on her worn-out body. So, she fell asleep with Youtube quietly playing in the background, filling the room with faint sounds.

Rena woke up around nine in the late evening to the familiar sensation of someone gently touching her. She moaned happily, her heart racing with surprise and delight. It had been such a long time since she had last seen him, and she realized just how much she truly missed him. Turning toward him, Rena was taken aback that she could actually see him so clearly.

"I thought I was going to go blind should I see you?" she exclaimed, half-jokingly. The first time they had met, she had instinctively known he was her soul—a duplicate of herself, though cloaked in darkness and mystery, and at that time, she couldn't see him at all. "Why can't I see you?" she remembered asking him in confusion.

"You will be blinded should you see me," he had told her, and she could still recall the way his body shook with a mix of mischief and laughter. Not knowing whether to believe him or doubt his words, but absolutely certain that she didn't want to risk losing her eyesight, she chose to drop the subject entirely. After all, no man or being was worth compromising her precious vision. So, she had settled for the sound of his voice, the warmth of his touch, and the intoxicating scent of him that lingered in the air.

She was no stranger to the experience of intimacy with invisible beings; it had become a common and curious aspect of her life since she turned eighteen. He was always there, a constant presence she thought she could trust without question. Yet, everything changed dramatically when he had mysteriously disappeared from her life for nearly eleven long years. He had faded into the background of her mind, becoming just another dream to her over time.

However, last year, after she had returned from her travels in Asia, he reappeared as if summoned back from wherever it was he had gone. Her traitorous soul had remembered him vividly, as if he had never really left her. He was back in her dreams, her thoughts, and her every waking moment, filling her heart once more with a blend of warmth and confusion.

Recently, after moving to the vibrant and bustling streets of Mexico City, she had begun to ignore him entirely. She convinced herself that she didn't want to have anything to do with him—or at least she tried very hard to believe that. In her mind, she placed the blame squarely on his shoulders for everything that had transpired. He was the source of her overwhelming passion that she struggled to control, the catalyst behind her decision to leave the church, and ultimately, the reason she had surrendered herself to that insufferable human, Behanzin.

It was only after crossing paths with Behanzin that she truly realized how desperately she longed for a genuine human relationship. His undeniably masculine presence gave her the fleeting hope that he could somehow conquer the intense, raging desires she harbored for that elusive being, the one she couldn't even see—her other half, her so-called soul. In the end, however, it turned out to be quite the bitter disappointment, leading her to withdraw completely into her own hermit zone. She found herself wanting to eliminate all those feelings entirely. She yearned to live free from the suffocating desperation and sought to forget everything she felt for the opposite sex. Yet now, here he was, so plain to see, and yet very different from the image she had created in her mind. She could clearly see his strikingly beautiful face, the warm honey color of his skin, and the straight shoulder-length raven-black hair that framed him. His eyes were a mesmerizing blend of violet and green, accentuating his chiseled jawline and strong chin.

But something was undeniably off about this entire situation. It was the peculiar scent that lingered mysteriously around him. He didn't possess the refreshing smell of sunshine and mountaintops, not even the faint, uplifting aroma of cut grass wafting through the summer breeze, nor the bracing scent of salted sea air that invigorated the soul. He lacked the familiar essence of sweat mingled with cedar wood or the fresh, revitalizing smell of clean raindrops on an early morning that usually brought comfort.

To her dismay and growing confusion, he didn't smell like her soul at all.

"You're not him," she exclaimed abruptly, sitting up as if jolted from a deep trance. "You're not him!" She reiterated in alarm, her eyes widening as she focused on the shadow moving stealthily in the dark. But if it wasn't him, then who in the world was this? She opened her mouth to scream, but before she could make a sound, she felt the shadow's warm hand clamped down over her mouth, silencing her. Her heart flipped with fear, pumping wildly in her chest.

"I am not the one you're thinking of. I am Twinnie," he told her, swinging his shoulder-length, straight, raven-black hair away from his face with an effortless motion, all while his hands still covered her mouth.

"Who?" she managed to mumble through the barrier of his hand.

"Your twin flame, Gerard," he replied smoothly. He finally released her, but his intense gaze suggested he was ready to clamp down on her again at a moment's notice.

"I have a twin flame?" she echoed, trying to process this astounding revelation.

"Yes, and I am he," he affirmed with a slight nod.

"Oh!" Rena sat there in stunned silence, gazing at the lovely male figure before her. His masculine energy stirred up feelings she had been desperately trying to ignore for the past eight long months.

As if reading her very thoughts, he slowly reached out for her, his hand gently caressing her delicate face. She harbored an overwhelming desire to purr like a contented cat, but in truth, he was not her Ori. Despite her conflicting feelings compelling her to push him away, she found herself irresistibly drawn to him, instinctively closing the space between them, rubbing against him in a feline manner, just as cats often rubbed up against the humans they adored.

"How long have we been twin flames?" she asked, seeking to distract herself from the whirlwind of sensations.

"For as long as you were created. Many millennia ago," he replied with a knowing look.

This revelation took her by surprise. She did not feel like an old soul steeped in history; instead, she felt young and, in many ways, foolish. Leaning her head against his shoulder for a fleeting moment, she drew in his vibrant energy while releasing the pent-up stress she had accumulated since her departure from Buffalo. An intoxicating sense of bliss enveloped her as she began to nuzzle her face against his neck, reveling in the warmth of his presence. He gently grasped her chin, halting her movements while bringing his face in close to hers. Without hesitation, she captured his lips in a fervent kiss, her soft moans filling the air.

Gerard, her twin flame, seemed to mirror her passionate intensity, igniting a fervor that she thought she had long buried. With each kiss, he reawakened the desires she had fought to keep at bay. Yet, for now, she surrendered to the consuming fire that ignited her senses.

He bent down to kiss her neck, his warm lips trailing over her skin, exploring their way down to her breast. There, he took one of her nipples into his warm mouth and suckled eagerly. The heat coursing through her was almost unbearable, and she craved nothing more than to feel his impressive bulge deep within her. But just as she thought he would give in to her desires, he slowly started to move away from her, leaving her breathless and yearning for more. One breast to the other, he took his time, deliberately ignoring her evident impatience. When he finally finished with one mound, he gently laid her back against the soft fabric beneath her and continued the journey of kissing slowly down to her navel, savoring each moment. There, he playfully stuck his tongue into the cute oval sink of her belly, teasing it briefly before shifting his focus to the place where Rena needed him the most…the place where desire truly ignited. He could clearly hear her soft moan escape her lips as he tantalizingly blew on her hot, yearning girly bit, sending exquisite shivers down her spine.

    Rena, feeling bold and utterly uninhibited, spread her legs completely, shamelessly inviting him to help himself to everything she had to offer. She felt his tongue fervently teasing her clitoris, its skilled movement deepening as it delved into her warmth, growing longer and harder, mirroring his manhood. Overwhelmed by sensation, Rena couldn't help but arch her back, holding his head firmly in place as he moved in and out with his golden tongue, each stroke electrifying her senses. Her legs seemed to want to open impossibly wide, as if desperate to welcome another wave of pleasure that was rapidly approaching.

Grasping his hair tightly, she held him to her as she screamed out in ecstasy. But her journey of bliss was far from over, and neither was his. He withdrew his tongue from her salty goodness to replace it with his firm manhood, flooding her with a sensation that sent her spiraling into another fiery frenzy. She swung one leg over his shoulder, fully wanting to take all of him deep inside her. He pounded her with relentless fervor, each thrust igniting a conflagration of feeling within her that signaled yet another impending release. But this time, she longed to truly savor every moment of her climax. Lowering her leg, she pressed them together while he leaned over her. His manhood never faltered, maintaining a steady rhythm as he slowly moved in and out. This particular position was undeniably his favorite, though Rena couldn't quite remember ever having forgotten the allure of it.

Closing her eyes, she slowly began to rotate her pelvis for him, savoring each deliberate movement, while he gradually moved in and out for her. They were both on fire, each lost in a captivating rhythm of their own making. Just as he was nearly at the edge of his release, he smoothly switched positions without disturbing the steady rhythm of his rotating manhood. His mouth captured hers fiercely, while her adventurous tongue eagerly devoured his in return. As her teeth sunk into his tongue, she could feel his release coincide with the overwhelming rush of pleasure that washed over her. Arching her back and still keeping her legs closed tightly around him, she could feel every exquisite inch of him as he drove in and out of her with intoxicating fervor. With her nails digging into the hardness of his taut buttocks, and her teeth biting down on his tongue, she held on to him as if her life depended on it, until the very ground beneath them shook violently, and she felt them both plummet into the deep, dark abyss of the earth's crust. There, amidst the chaos, their screams echoed through the crevices and cracks of the cavernous depths. As the earthquake finally subsided, they found themselves back in the bathroom, lying exhausted on the makeshift bed on the floor. Tired and translucent, she felt him gently roll off of her to her side. Turning to face him, she instinctively curled her frame around him. Rena watched as he propped himself up on his elbow, gazing intently into her eyes.

"Be careful," he instructed softly, a hint of concern lacing his tone.

"Be careful of what?" she asked, curiosity piquing in her voice.

"Just be careful," he replied, his expression serious yet tender.

The ominous warning did not seem to register in her mind, nor did it curb her intense desires. She craved the exhilarating feeling of him again.

Boldly, she took his free hand and expertly guided his two middle fingers to her lips, where she sensually sucked on them, savoring each moment slowly, before directing them to her wet womanhood. There, she eagerly inserted them deep inside her. Her eyes never wavered from his beautifully captivating face as she slowly began to rotate on his fingers, relishing every sensation. She didn't want to grasp the meaning of his warning, nor did she want the thrilling night to come to an end. She just wanted to continue having her way with him throughout the night and perhaps into the next day.

Gerard was fully aware of her desires, and he willingly allowed her to have her way with his fingers. When she was fully aroused and noticed his throbbing shaft had hardened in response to her actions, Rena turned her back to him, arching her beautifully curved buttocks invitingly for him to enter her. He didn't move as she expected him to, so with a subtle urgency, she reached between her legs, grasping him and inserting him inside her. He rose behind her, pulling her up onto her hands and knees, forcefully spreading her legs apart with his knees, claiming her completely. She felt him grip both of her hips tightly, then glide both of his large hands to her butt cheeks, squeezing them hard and getting a deliciously good look at her enticing pinky goodness before thrusting his hard cock deep into her, the intense fire blazed within them both.

She opened her legs wider, arching her back and giving him everything she had to offer. She craved more of him, his warmth, his power, and the connection they shared. Hearing her innermost thoughts, he responded by ramming into her harder and faster, determined to drive his manhood as deeply inside her as he possibly could.

Where was he when she so desperately needed to be pleasured like this in Buffalo? Suddenly, he was no longer inside her, and she found herself crouching on her hands and knees, back arched enticingly with her pussy exposed, eagerly waiting for him to continue driving himself into her. But to her dismay, nothing happened.

Where was that cock she longed for? Looking back over her shoulder to see what he was doing, she was met only with the stark bathroom wall, devoid of his presence.

"Fuck it!" she exclaimed in frustration. She sank down onto her makeshift bed, curling into herself, thoughts racing as she processed how surreal this moment felt. The urge to finish the deed herself was overwhelming, but her exhaustion was even greater. Giving in to fatigue, she drifted off to sleep with her twin flame firmly on her mind, the lingering traces of desire still dancing in her thoughts.

The Jamaican

Chapter 5
THE BIRDS OF THE TREES

Rena woke up to the delightful sound of hundreds of birds chirping and flitting around, re-situating themselves in their nests to greet and embrace the warm rays of the morning sun.

The sexy dream she had enjoyed the previous night lingered in her mind, prompting her fingers to absentmindedly reach for her wet groin. However, she quickly reminded herself that she didn't want to start that alluring activity again. It would only lead her back into temptation, a temptation that she had consciously left behind in Buffalo. With a frown, she turned her face into the soft, fluffy pillow and groaned quietly, before forcing her mind to focus instead on the vibrant sounds coming from outside her window.

Her thoughts began to flicker and flutter like the birds, landing on random imaginative ideas, such as the whimsical concept of a house that could talk. The notion of a talking house brought a laugh bubbling up, causing her to giggle at the absurdity of that idea. But on second thought, it was not so absurd at all. The colorful birds had a special relationship with their houses—the trees they called home. So engrossed was she in this playful contemplation that she effectively diverted her attention away from her feminine parts, delaying her realization that a tiny sparrow was shrieking insistently for her attention.

"Isn't it a bit too early for all that noise?" she questioned, slightly annoyed. She lay there, attempting to ignore its incessant chattering, but soon enough, a second sparrow flew to the same spot, and together they continued their chorus—this time even louder.

~~~~~~~~~~

Rena had long since discovered, through her many observations, that the birds were indeed in cahoots with the trees surrounding her temporary home. Her friends Nuck, Tuck, and the others had taken to using the poor little creatures to get her attention whenever they found themselves bored and seeking some amusement. She learned this odd little truth months ago when a persistent sparrow came to her window, making quite the ruckus that was hard to ignore. She knew instinctively that it was not carrying a message meant specifically for her, given the intensity of the bird's tweeting. The poor little creature sounded decidedly more aggravated than anything else.

Feeling a surge of curiosity and concern, she hurriedly got up and rushed to the window to see what was bothering it so much. However, to her dismay, it flew away the very moment she reached the window, as if it had simply been waiting for her to approach. "Hmm, I guess it's okay," she thought to herself, trying to dismiss the nagging feeling. She had gone back to the bathroom to immerse herself once more in her YouTube videos. Yet, moments later, the sparrow returned, shrieking insistently. It puzzled Rena significantly that the bird was repeatedly coming back to her window to insistently shriek.

Once again, she reluctantly left her video behind to return to the window, but, predictably, the little thing flew off once more before she could catch a glimpse. A wave of worry washed over her for the small bird. What if it had caught Covid? She was just learning that animals could catch the disease, too, and the thought made her uneasy. She watched intently as it flew away, noticing nothing particularly out of the ordinary in its movements or demeanor.

She had seen that her friends were trying incredibly hard to maintain a straight face, and this realization made her all the more concerned for the little sparrow. The tiny creature flew away only to return repeatedly with its incessant, attention-seeking shrieking each time she vanished into the bathroom.

"Y'all really need to stop the playing," she had told them sternly, shaking her finger at them with a hint of annoyance, especially when she saw just how hard they were trying not to laugh. But instead of taking her seriously, they had responded by laughing even harder at her distress. It was at that moment she became acutely aware that the small birds were merely doing the bidding of her friends, an unwitting part of their elaborate joke. Although the frequency of the sparrow's shrieking at her window had lessened somewhat, her friends were still sending the birds whenever they felt the need to entertain themselves.

~~~~~~~

Rena, eventually, got up and quietly walked over to the large window. The two sparrows, perched nearby, immediately ceased their lively chattering, turned their tiny heads to gaze at her, and then looked back at the unmoving trees outside, before gladly taking flight and soaring off to their hidden quarters. They fluttered off into the thick, darkened foliage of the trees, where the others—hundreds, possibly thousands, of their feathered companions—of many different species—were already settled in, preparing to greet the rising sun with their melodious calls. She cast a glance over at the trees and noticed that even Sarai, her ever-curious friend, had her eyes glued to the window, probably wondering where Rena had disappeared to and why she had not yet made her way to the window to greet the sun.

Did they somehow know of her recent sexy dreams? She couldn't help but wonder. The golden sun was rising majestically over the building, illuminating everything with its warm glow. The birds' anticipation created a palpable energy, and she could feel it humming in the air. The early morning sun was bathing the entire scene in a stunning rose gold light—including the quirky zinc roof of the hotel garage, which glinted under the gentle rays. She had never witnessed the sun display such an enchanting hue before—not even during her time living in Jamaica. It made her ponder deeply about what was going to happen next in her life.

She looked up at her friends towering impressively over the majestic eighteenth-century red brick building, which was uniquely shaped in the form of a boot from her vantage point. The old man, whom she had become accustomed to seeing frequently, appeared shirtless on the rooftop, oblivious to the unique world around him . The trees that surrounded the building immediately lost their distinctive facial

The Jamaican

features, now looking like just any ordinary evergreen trees. Rena pretended not to notice the man and instead shifted her gaze skyward at the breathtaking rose gold clouds, a captivating optical illusion brought on by the rising sun's warm embrace.

With a sigh, she moved away from the window, effectively closed the curtains, and secured them tightly with her trusty clothes pin. The man was undeniably elderly, and she assumed he might be the owner of the building itself. During her first week of moving into the hotel, she had awoken in the early morning, only to find him on the rooftop, peering through the window into her room, silently watching her as she slept, she imagined. That unsettling moment was when she had decided to start closing the curtains firmly at night. Occasionally, he would be seen there with a family member, who could be either a small boy or a younger female, creating an odd tableau that lingered in her mind.

Rena had once asked her close friends if he was, in fact, a bad man, during that unsettling first time she had seen him interacting with the younger people. They had quickly reassured her that he was okay, insisting that he meant no harm. Half an hour later, feeling a mix of curiosity and concern, she turned off the light and returned to the window, peering out into the twilight. To her surprise, the old man was gone, as if he had simply vanished into thin air. She looked at her friends, whose glowing white auras shone brightly against the enchanting rose gold sky, making it increasingly difficult for her to clearly make out their reflections in the dim light. Rena knew, however, that they could see her just fine.

"*Thank you again for saving that boy,*" she said to Sarai, suddenly remembering the strikingly beautiful boy and the urgency of the moment.

~~~~~~~~

Rena had long since known that trees could talk, a secret she cherished deeply. Years ago, when she had lived on Post Avenue in the enchanting city of Rochester, Upstate New York, she had first heard them chattering in a way that had forever altered her perception of nature. It was early evening, the blissful beginning of summer, and she had been making her way to the backyard, where the trash and recyclables were kept, intending to dispose of her kitchen waste.

"She's emptying her garbage," she distinctly heard as if the trees were gossiping among themselves. The voice was not human; it resonated more like a soft whispering chime carried by the gentle wind.

"Who's that?" she recalled asking, her curiosity piqued, while nervously looking up into the trees, her heart racing fiercely. The energy emanating from the trees heightened her senses, and the sudden, eerie silence of the birds and the lone butterfly added to the atmosphere of mystery surrounding her.

For a fleeting moment, everything had come to a standstill, wrapping her in an intensely eerie feeling that sent shivers down her spine and raised the hairs on her arms and neck. With her heart pounding wildly, she turned her gaze toward the trees above, anticipating the sight of some ethereal creature or figure, yet all she found were the abundant, compacted foliage of two giant trees whose expansive branches had intertwined, forming what appeared to be one colossal tree that cast a shadow over her like nature's protective cloak.

A gentle breeze was blowing softly, causing the sunlight to flicker in and out playfully through the rustling leaves above her. The lingering eerie feeling she had initially experienced persisted, intensified by the overwhelming energy of an unseen, non-human presence that she had never sensed in this familiar place before. With her heart pounding in her chest and her steps quickened by an instinctual urge to flee, she hurriedly made her way to the garbage disposal area, swiftly dumped her trash, and rushed back to the perceived safety of the building.

The moment she closed the entrance door securely behind her, everything outside seemed to revert to its usual normalcy. The sweet singing and cheerful chirping of the birds resumed, while the playful squirrels busily cracked the shells of their nuts, some of them even playfully squabbling with one another over their prized snacks. Although she had never again heard that unsettling sound, the frightening sensation of a non-human presence was always palpable every time she ventured into the backyard to discard her garbage.

Only recently had Rena come to the realization that she had inadvertently tapped into the unique dimension and frequency of the trees surrounding her home. It was a phenomenon that the birds had instinctively performed since the dawn of time. She had learned that Quantum Theory, a subject she didn't know much about, suggested the existence of multiple dimensions on Earth waiting to be discovered. These dimensions were layered within one another, each resonating at its own frequency. For a fleeting moment, she had tapped into the trees' dimension on Post Avenue without even realizing it. Instead, she had tormented herself with the belief that she was losing her grip on reality. Now, here she was, years later, capable of engaging in genuine conversations with those ancient beings.

The Jamaican

Chapter 6
THE HOTEL CATALINA'S MAID

The lights were off, shrouding the small space in darkness, and Rena found herself lying on her back with her feet flat against the cool, tiled surface of her makeshift bed, positioned on the bathroom floor. The night air was biting cold, resulting in her skin and scalp starting to itch uncontrollably. She had always suffered from an intensely itchy scalp, yet it was only recently that her skin had begun to react similarly, with irritation more pronounced than before. This peculiar situation had commenced back in July when she had experienced her very first snowfall in the bustling metropolis of Mexico City.

"A freak snowstorm," they had classified it adamantly on the News. During that time, she had been staying at a different hotel, The Hotel Catalina, where she had unwittingly become embroiled in an unusual situation. At first, Rena believed that her discomfort might be due to the actions of one of the maids who had returned from the pandemic lockdown. A woman who seemingly observed her presence and immediately took a strong disliking to her. The energy radiating from the woman was so overtly negative that Rena felt compelled to adopt an excessively pleasant demeanor whenever the woman was near, hoping to diffuse the mounting tension.

Rena, who had been living at The Catalina Hotel for more than two months with the generous monetary assistance of a long-time friend, found herself in a somewhat precarious situation. Although she was sometimes late with her payment, she always made sure to pay her bills in full. This had presented no problem to Alberto, the hardworking hotel manager and receptionist, who appreciated her presence. With the hotel experiencing low occupancy rates, he was genuinely happy to have her there, especially since she was a guest who provided her own cleaning benefits. While she didn't mind taking care of her own living space, including the bathroom, she always found herself having to ask for the necessary cleaning supplies, which could be a bit inconvenient.

Over the last couple of days, Rena had started to notice some distinct changes in Alberto's attitude, particularly following the recent return of another woman to the hotel. These changes became more pronounced as each day passed. However, Rena did not take this shift in demeanor personally, as she believed it was simply a reflection of the circumstances around them. On her final day there, Rena picked up the hotel phone and rang for Alberto.

"Hello," he answered, sounding breathless, as if he had been busy with other tasks.

"Hi Alberto, can you please send someone up with a broom, if possible?"

"Sure, no problem at all, just give me a couple of minutes to find someone," he assured her.

"Okay, thank you."

Rena had recently spoken to him about the troubling money situation and had made a firm promise to pay him back the very next day, but her room hadn't been thoroughly swept in quite some time. This realization prompted her to decide to do a quick cleaning before she treated herself to a refreshing shower. Additionally, she also needed the broom to properly wash the bathroom floor, which was in dire need of attention. When the knock on the door came a few minutes later, she certainly wasn't expecting the unpleasant woman on the other side. Rena forced a smile anyway to mask her surprise. However, that smile quickly faded as she glimpsed the filthy broom and rusty, dirty dustpan the woman had brought for her to use in her room. Rena's mind raced with the horrifying thought of catching COVID-19 just from looking at those tools. For such a beautifully maintained hotel, the sight of the dirty broom and dustpan was so revolting that she immediately scrunched up her face in disgust.

"I can't use that," she blurted out impulsively, waving the woman away with a dismissive gesture.

A few hours later, her phone rang, and it was Alberto calling to ask for the money she owed him. This was a bold move as he had never made such a direct request before.

"I have to go to Western Union to pick it up," she replied, trying to maintain her composure.

She had hurriedly dressed and left the hotel with uncertainty lingering in her mind, fully aware that she wouldn't have been able to pay him, especially since she hadn't heard anything from her friend in days. By the time she returned in the late evening, the weight of her situation felt heavier than ever.

"I'm really sorry about this, Alberto, but unfortunately, the money just wasn't available at Western Union, and I have been diligently trying to call all the contacts I know here, but so far, I have had no success. Can you possibly give me another night?"

"Yes, but you have to leave tomorrow if I don't receive the payment," he had threatened her unpleasantly, his tone leaving no room for negotiation.

Rena felt a wave of relief wash over her. Her phone minutes had completely run out, and she desperately needed access to the hotel's internet to reach out to her friend in Rochester. That night, she was genuinely overjoyed when her friend had, albeit reluctantly, agreed to send her some much-needed money.

"I can't be paying your hotel bill all the time. You should really consider getting a job," he had said, completely unaware of the challenging situation she was currently facing.

"I am trying, Luke. I'm really trying, but the conditions here have gotten even worse for the locals. Schools have all closed down. Everything has shifted online, and unfortunately, my computer has been hit with an insidious bug that is preventing me from doing anything productive online. They are only hiring a limited number of people now since the economy is so unstable."

"Can't you look for something different? Maybe find a cleaning job or something similar?" he suggested, his lack of understanding clear.

"Nobody wants to hire someone like me. This is Mexico. There are countless locals who need jobs," she had told him, speaking the truth while detesting the way he minimized her education, seeing her only as someone who cleans other people's dirty floors. However, she kept her thoughts to herself. She was, after all, in a position of need, effectively a beggar, and had to play the part well, even if it meant kissing his ass.

"Well, let me know when you get something, because I don't have it like that to keep helping you." He said this with a hint of frustration in his voice.

"Okay," she had responded, feeling a wave of gratitude wash over her despite the words.

He was not Behanzin, but in many ways, he was just as much of an insufferable ass, too. She was able to pay Alberto for the services rendered, and fortunately, she had enough left over for another couple of nights at the least. She had started breathing a little easier, again, allowing herself a moment of relief.

That night she had taken a long, soothing shower and settled into bed. However, once in bed, her skin suddenly felt like it was on fire with an alarming intensity. The itching she felt was unlike anything she had ever gone through in her life. She started scratching feverishly all over her body, desperate to find some relief, but feeling like she couldn't scratch fast enough to ease the torment. Rena didn't know how long she stood there in an agonizing frenzy of scratching, but when her hands finally grew tired of the relentless itch, she looked down at her nails; they were filled with blood, and she felt a wave of alarm wash over her.

"Drink two spoons of apple cider vinegar," something inside her urged decisively. Without hesitation, she bounced off the bed to retrieve the bottle of vinegar and hurriedly took the remedy. A minute later, the intensity of the itching slowly began to diminish, allowing her to feel considerably better. To ensure her bed was clean, she decided to run her hands over the sheets before climbing back into it, only to feel some salt-like gravel scattered across the fabric. Suddenly, a face appeared in her line of vision, and she blurted out, "That fucking bitch!"

Walking over to her suitcase to extract the king-size sheet she had thoughtfully packed for this trip, she felt a sense of relief wash over her. She spread it out meticulously on top of the bed—using it as an essential protective barrier between her and the questionable hotel sheets. The next morning, she groggily woke up, splashed some cool water on her face, and brushed her teeth with renewed vigor before heading downstairs to pay Alberto for her stay. Her skin was now stinging and burning from the aggressive scratching she had given it the previous night, but she chose to ignore the discomfort. Downstairs, she spotted the dreadful woman standing far too close to Alberto, which led her to believe the two were potentially involved in some sort of relationship.

"Good morning, Alberto. How are you?" she asked, trying to keep her tone light.

"I'm good," he replied, not looking up from his tasks.

"Can I get the room for another night?" she inquired, hopeful yet apprehensive.

"Sorry, you have to check out today; we need the room," he said, his voice firm.

"Do you have anything cheaper?" she promptly asked, her heart racing at the prospect. Maybe they might have a more affordable option available.

"No, we are completely booked out," he replied with finality.

Rena was taken aback by this news. She glanced over at the gloating hotel maid who stood nearby and caught the triumphant look in her eyes before she dramatically turned her back and walked out of Alberto's office.

"Check out is at eleven a.m.," he informed her with a distasteful look etched on his face, indicating that her time was running out.

"I had the money to pay you for another night," Rena had pleaded desperately, trying hard not to let him see her alarmed shaking hands, which were betraying her anxiety. She watched him shake his head, unbendingly, like a statue that had long ago forgotten warmth.

"The borders are open now. The room you are occupying was part of a promotional offer. That promotion has come to an end, so unless you have the original price to pay for it, I'm afraid you cannot stay," he informed her, his tone final and devoid of empathy.

"How much is it?" she asked, holding on to a glimmer of hope.

"It's fifteen hundred pesos," he told her flatly, knowing full well that she didn't have that kind of money to spare. "Be out at eleven," he repeated, his gaze unyielding and impersonal.

Rena felt utterly devastated at the sudden change in him. Just two months earlier, he had been the only person she had been conversing with, sharing laughter and stories that kept the loneliness at bay. He had always been such a charming and pleasant man, radiating warmth and kindness. Yet all that pleasantness and charm had evaporated as if they had never existed. In its place was this cold and unfeeling person who now stood before her, leaving her heart to sink deeper in despair, wondering what had caused this unexpected transformation in him.

"Why?" she finally managed to ask, her voice barely a whisper.

"That room is expensive, so we need it to rent out to other visitors," he replied, his tone leaving no room for negotiation.

"Oh, so it's not me then, you just needed the room?" She remembered asking, her mind racing with thoughts of the news she had watched the night before, where the Mexican President had announced plans to re-open the borders for tourism. She thought of that and chose to believe him, clinging to the hope that perhaps things would return to normal soon.

"We need the room, so be out by eleven," he stated again, the finality in his voice echoing in the now silent space between them.

She went back upstairs with a heavy heart, burdened by thoughts weighing on her mind, but considering her situation, it could have been much worse. At least she had the option to rent a more affordable space. With a sense of gratitude, she thanked the Great Mother for continuously looking out for her well-being. After taking a refreshing shower, she dressed thoughtfully, made herself breakfast, and efficiently packed her belongings for the day ahead. By the time noon arrived, she was out of the room, dragging her heavy suitcases behind her with determination.

When she finally reached the small lobby, her eyes fell upon the maid, who stood there with a look that was both evil and triumphant. At that moment, Rena understood what had really taken place behind the scenes. They were living in critical times, filled with challenges that seemed hard to navigate. Rena learned, during her experience here in Mexico City, that not everybody welcomed people like her with open arms. It was disheartening how easily people's attitudes could switch from good to bad in an instant. This inconsistency made her wonder if there had ever truly been good intentions in the first place.

She resolved to force the negative thoughts from her mind while she stood outside the hotel, anxiously waiting for the taxi she had asked Alberto to call for her. Shortly thereafter, an unmarked vehicle pulled up in front of her, its appearance raising a flicker of concern.

"Is this the taxi?" she called out, pushing her head through the door to ask Alberto, whose energy still felt heavy and negative. Nevertheless, he managed to respond to her inquiry politely.

"Yes!" he affirmed.

"Thank you," she replied, cautiously stepping forward to take control of her day.

He didn't respond at all; instead, he simply picked up the phone, doing so in a distinctly dismissive manner. Meanwhile, the taxi driver emerged from his vehicle and went out of his way to help her load her bags and belongings into the trunk of the car. Rena couldn't shake off her growing concern that the large black Sedan taxi seemed somewhat dangerous, making her feel uneasy, so she whispered a prayer to the Great Mother, hoping she would keep her safe during this unsettling experience.

Less than ten minutes later, the taxi finally pulled up in front of the hotel she had carefully booked. To her dismay, the driver charged her three times the amount that it had cost to get there. It was a classic case of bad people pretending to be good until proven undeniably bad. She reluctantly paid the driver and tried to put both The Catalina Hotel and Alberto far out of her mind, hoping to find some peace of mind.

The Jamaican

"THE TREES MAY NOT HAVE EYES LIKE US, BUT THEY'RE SEEING EVERYTHING, EVEN THE DUST."

"THE TREES MAY NOT HAVE EARS LIKE US, BUT THEY'RE LISTENING TO EVERYTHING, EVEN WHEN WE FIGHT AND CUSS."

"THE TREES MAY NOT HAVE MOUTH LIKE US, BUT THEY EAT, SPEAK AND NEVER MAKE FUSS."

"THE TREES MAY NOT HAVE FEET LIKE US, BUT THEY'RE WALKING, EVEN WHILE YOU CATCH THE BUS."

Chapter 7
THE NEW HOTEL

She was warmly greeted in the bustling parking lot of Universales by Alphonso, a striking figure with Aztec features, who appeared to be of Mexican descent. He was tall, strapping, and quite pleasant-looking, exuding a friendly demeanor. With a smile, he took her heavy suitcases, which seemed to weigh a ton, and effortlessly carried them to the lobby while checking her in with efficiency and grace.

Rena had made her booking through Bookings for a stay of four days, and she felt a wave of relief wash over her, realizing she still had some money left over for a couple more nights if she chose that option. In her heart, she knew that things had worked out for the best despite the bumps in the road. She resolutely refused to feel guilty about the way her time had ended with The Hotel Catalina. Although the quality of the new hotel was a significant step down from the previous one, it was comfortable enough and much more affordable, which was a relief during her travels.

Unfortunately, the four days at the new hotel did little to improve her sleep quality. The incessant noise of traffic filtering through the window kept her awake long into the night, something she simply wasn't used to after her previous, quieter accommodations. After much contemplation, Rena decided to book an Airbnb she found online that was available for the same price. This delightful find offered her the entire space to herself, complete with a full kitchen and a washing machine—everything she had wanted for her stay. The Airbnb was conveniently located near the hotel, making it an ideal choice. As she made her decision to walk to her new lodging, she left her bags with Alphonso, who was curious to know why she was choosing to leave the hotel.

"The room was noisy and I wasn't able to sleep," she explained.

"You should have told me; I would have changed the room for you. We have many empty rooms here," he replied, his tone genuinely concerned.

"Since I already booked the Airbnb for two days, I'll come back," Rena had promised, hoping he would understand her choice.

The washing machine, along with the entire kitchen area, at the new Airbnb was urgently calling out to her, prompting her to take action. She really, desperately needed to do some laundry; her current method of washing her clothes by hand was something she had always found utterly tedious and unpleasant. Moreover, there was no comparison between hand washing and using a machine—the washing machine, in her opinion, simply did a far superior job at getting clothes clean.

It took her an entire hour to locate the place, navigating through unfamiliar streets. When she finally arrived, her disappointment was overwhelming and immediate. There were two enormous pit bulls lounging around, and she couldn't help but wonder if she had overlooked any mention of pets in the listings on Bookings. To make matters worse, the washing machine was situated in the same cramped and unkempt space where the garbage was kept, which she found utterly disgusting. She had even caught a glimpse of the owners still cleaning the rooms, and the oppressive smell of bleach that filled the air almost made her gag. The sofa chair was so filthy and tattered that it looked like it had originally belonged in a garbage pile, right next to the washing machine. Rena could also hear the furious coughing of someone nearby, which only added to her discomfort, making it clear that the hotel was definitely safer and more comfortable.

"I'm sorry, but this doesn't look at all like what I saw on Bookings," she asserted firmly to the young man who had greeted her. "I simply can't stay here."

"Okay," was all he replied, accompanied by a careless shrug of his bony shoulders, which only deepened her frustration.

After returning to the Universales, she promptly sent an email to Bookings detailing the dismal condition of the Airbnb and explaining her reasons for not being able to stay there. In response, Bookings sent her a tax refund but unfortunately did not include a refund for the two nights of the room. Instead, they instructed her to reach out to the Airbnb owners directly for further assistance.

She dialled the Airbnb number, her fingers trembling slightly with frustration.

"Hello," came the voice on the other end.

"Hi, this is Rena. I was just at your Airbnb a short while ago. I called Bookings, and they told me to contact you directly regarding my refund, since the space I received wasn't adequately portrayed on the website."

"I'm sorry, but we have a strict no refund policy," the voice replied, devoid of compassion.

"Mother footloose!" Rena blurted out in disbelief. She hadn't noticed that detail in the fine print, and she scolded herself for her oversight. "But that was my last twenty dollars! What am I going to do now?" she pleaded, attempting to evoke some sympathy from the man on the line.

"No refund!" He confirmed, his tone turning curt, and before she could respond further, he abruptly slammed the phone down on her.

No refund. Now she understood why they seemed so relieved when she informed them of her departure; they had quite effectively earned themselves an easy twenty bucks. Feeling defeated, Rena went back onto Bookings to verify this disheartening information, and sure enough, there it was—the dreaded no refund policy, along with the notifications about pet dogs on the premises she had completely overlooked. She really needed to pay closer attention to these seemingly little details, as they were what had gotten her into this unfortunate predicament in the first place, she sighed in resignation.

The forty-five-minute walk back to the Universales had provided some clarity, clearing her head somewhat, but now, as she trudged along, she was feeling less positive than before.

She was sitting quietly in the common area of the orange building, lost in thought about her unfortunate loss of twenty dollars when she caught sight of Alphonso coming down the stairs with one of the hotel staff, who was diligently carrying an orange bucket filled with soapy water and a mop.

"How was it?" he asked curiously, pausing for a moment to engage with her.

"Very disappointing," she responded dejectedly, her tone reflecting her frustration. She had truly been looking forward to the convenience of doing all her laundry in the washing machine, which would have saved her both time and effort. Unfortunately, the Universales hotel didn't offer laundry facilities for the guests, so she began mentally preparing herself to wash everything by hand in the cramped bathroom.

Alphonso looked at her with sympathetic eyes, and she appreciated that kind gesture.

"Would you like me to show you the rooms we have available?" he offered with a hint of hopefulness.

"Yes, but give me just a minute. I have to make a few important calls first," Rena told him, wanting to stay focused on her tasks.

"Sure, take your time," he replied kindly.

Rena moved over to the wooden bench situated conveniently by one of the rooms, just a couple of meters away from the receptionist area. She dialed Luke's number, praying fervently that he would pick up the phone this time.

"Hello," came the voice on the other end, sounding both authoritarian and no-nonsense. She felt a wave of relief wash over her that he had answered so promptly.

"I had to leave that hotel for something cheaper," she informed him, carefully avoiding any mention of the fact that she had ultimately been kicked out. He didn't need to know those details. Luke had always hated spending money, even when he had it abundantly rolling in. It surprised Rena that he had been willing to help her for this long. But now, she couldn't shake the feeling that he was preparing to pull back his assistance.

"How much cheaper?" He inquired, his curiosity getting the better of him.

"It's eleven dollars a night here," she replied without hesitation.

"Okay," he said, and then promptly hung up the phone. Just two minutes later, a notification pinged on her phone, and she saw that he had sent her seventy-five dollars. With a heart now filled with relief, she returned to the receptionist area and confidently booked another five nights with Universales. She had specifically requested a room that would be away from the noisy traffic, one that featured windows looking directly at lush green trees. Alphonso was kind enough to take her to three different rooms that fit within the budget she had arranged, until they ultimately settled on a nice room located in front of a building on the second floor. The views of the many trees made her very thankful. Her window was situated right above the roof of the hotel's entryway. While she supposed it would do for now, she couldn't help but hope for something a little cozier.

~~~~~~~

The first night she reluctantly slept in the cramped room, the incessant itching had returned with a vengeance, attacking her skin like a bothersome pest. In a desperate attempt to find relief, she took a long, soothing shower and then applied a generous amount of lotion to her irritated body, hoping it might quell the incessant discomfort. However, her skin stubbornly refused to cooperate, continuing its relentless assault of itching. To make matters worse, the disturbing sounds of two men in the room directly adjacent to hers, coupled with the unmistakable smell of anal sex, intruded upon her desperate scratching frenzy, intensifying her unease.

Recalling the vinegar remedy from The Catalina Hotel, she headed to the makeshift kitchen and treated herself to a couple spoonfuls, hoping for the often magical relief it had provided before. While the itching lessened slightly, it did not disappear as completely as it had on previous occasions.

Rena had never witnessed two men engaging in such acts before, leading her mind to entertain the possibility that someone was merely watching a particularly raucous scene of porn. However, that thought was quickly extinguished when the noises of their activity resonated quite loudly against the thin, connecting wall.

The unmistakably intimate sounds continued on and on throughout the long night, making it nearly impossible for her to find any semblance of peace. In a desperate measure, she stuffed tissues into her ears, attempting to lessen the overwhelming noise while simultaneously suffering through the vile smell and the unbearable itching that plagued her, fighting the urge to scream in frustration. By the next day, with a tired body and an itchy demeanor, Rena resolved to go get something stronger for her troubled skin at the local pharmacy. As she made her way down the stairs, she unexpectedly crossed paths with Alphonso.

"Did you hear?" he asked, his voice tinged with urgency.

"Hear what?" she replied, her curiosity piqued.

"The President has decided to keep the borders closed indefinitely."

"It's a smart move," she responded thoughtfully.

"Money is absolutely necessary to run a country, but it cannot be effectively run by the dead and the sick."

Alphonso nodded his head in agreement at that notion.

"I'm going for a walk; I'll see you later," she informed him, feeling a mix of anticipation and desire for fresh air.

"Okay, Rena, just be careful out there," he cautioned.

"Yes, I will, thank you," she assured him with a smile. Waving goodbye to Alphonso, she made her exit from the comforting surroundings.

She was feeling a profound sense of relief for having chosen to stay at the Universales. The staff there were treating her like family, rather than just another guest. Her mind momentarily wandered to The Hotel Catalina, and she let out a soft sigh, pondering the contrasts and memories associated with it.

The President had decisively retracted his previous order for the re-opening of the borders, primarily due to the alarming pandemic death rate and the continuous, widespread transmission of the virus. As a direct result of this decision, a significant number of hotels found themselves forced to cancel numerous bookings, which left many travelers feeling stranded and anxious. Consequently, a great many people were sent back home, turning their travel plans into a frustrating experience. She sighed, feeling the weight of the situation, again.

At the pharmacy, which was conveniently located not more than a five-minute walk away from the hotel, she quickly accessed the Google Translate app on her phone to craft a simple inquiry in Spanish. After carefully translating her question, she handed the phone to one of the assistants working there. The assistant kindly took her by the hand and guided her to the particular aisle where the various body oils meant for relieving itching were prominently displayed. Rena was pleasantly surprised by the vast selection available. The assistant picked up the most expensive product on the shelf and handed it to her with a smile. Rena examined the label closely, read through the instructions, and ultimately decided to put it back on the shelf, feeling it wasn't what she needed.

"I'll look around until I find something more suitable," she translated on her phone to communicate her intentions.

"Okay," the assistant replied cheerfully before walking away to assist other customers.

"Muchos gracias," Rena expressed her gratitude as the assistant departed.

"De nada," the assistant replied warmly.

Rena carefully went over all the selections available to her, weighing the options thoughtfully, but in the end, she ultimately chose the most affordable items that fit within her budget. She picked up a few food items to cook simple meals during her stay. It would have definitely been cheaper if she had made the effort to go to the supermarket, which was conveniently located only a thirty-minute walk away from her current location. However, she unfortunately didn't feel like walking in the hot sun—even though it was unusually cool for that time of the year, a welcome relief in many ways. After paying for her selected items and a large bottle of water to keep herself hydrated, she returned to her hotel room in hopes of finding a little peace and quiet so she could get some much-needed rest.

"THE TREES MAY NOT HAVE EYES LIKE US, BUT THEY'RE SEEING EVERYTHING, EVEN THE DUST."

"THE TREES MAY NOT HAVE EARS LIKE US, BUT THEY'RE LISTENING TO EVERYTHING, EVEN WHEN WE FIGHT AND CUSS."

"THE TREES MAY NOT HAVE MOUTH LIKE US, BUT THEY EAT, SPEAK AND NEVER MAKE FUSS."

"THE TREES MAY NOT HAVE FEET LIKE US, BUT THEY'RE WALKING, EVEN WHILE YOU CATCH THE BUS."

CHAPTER 8
GO FIND A MAN

Rena was now well into her third week at the hotel. The relentless itching she felt had gotten increasingly worse, becoming an unbearable nuisance. The bottle of oil she had purchased, which gave her a glimmer of hope, had tragically stopped working effectively after just the second application. She was doing her utmost not to become consumed with worry about her declining health and increasingly dire situation. However, this was proving to be a difficult feat to achieve. She hadn't managed to pay the hotel bill in over a week, and her supplies were dwindling down to just a little bit of flour and a small amount of oil left in the bottom of the bottle. What on earth was she going to do? Luke had mysteriously stopped answering his phone, leaving her feeling even more isolated. To add to her misery, the private room she occupied was exposing her to all the goings-on around her, amplifying her sense of entrapment.

The intrusive sounds of risqué activities had gotten worse, echoing through the thin walls. Some mornings, when she reluctantly got up to empty her overflowing garbage, she would bear witness to teenage boys leaving the rooms of their older male lovers—some displaying guilt and disgust plastered all over their youthful faces, while others seemed to walk away with an undeserved sense of triumph.

She had long since concluded that the hotel was more of a brothel than an actual hotel. It wasn't attracting any foreign guests; instead, it only offered its services to local men who were indulging in the call girl and male services available within its worn-down walls. Occasionally, she would also hear the heart-wrenching cries of children being scolded by the adult men she assumed were their fathers. Despite the distressing sounds surrounding her, she tried not to put much focus on it; she had far too many pressing problems of her own to deal with.

It had been nearly seven long days since Luke had finally stopped answering his phone altogether. Deep down, Rena knew in her heart that Luke was purposely ignoring her calls, but a small part of her clung to the hope that perhaps he still harbored some goodness in his heart for her. After all, the entire globe was grappling with an unprecedented crisis, and he was practically loaded with money. Would he really allow her to suffer and potentially die during her time of desperate need? She didn't want to consider the terrifying possibility that he might have caught COVID-19, especially since she had been watching the news report countless people dying across the United States from the devastating disease.

Suddenly, a firm knock sounded on her door, causing her heart to skip a beat in response. She hurried to open it, revealing Rosa, one of the kind-hearted hotel maids.

"Buenos Dias! Can you go downstairs to the office please?" Rena didn't even need to ask why; she already had a gut feeling about the situation.

"Okay, I'll be there shortly," she replied with resignation.

"Esta bien," Rosa said softly before turning and walking away. Rena closed the door, her mind racing, and quickly changed her clothes and brushed her teeth. Intense fear began to gnaw at her heart, filled with anxious thoughts. Were they going to put her out? How on earth had she ended up in this dismal situation? No friends, no family members, absolutely no one to help her during her most desperate times of need. With a heavy heart, she made her way to the office where Alphonso was seated, waiting for her arrival.

"Is everything okay with you?" he asked, his voice laced with concern.

"Not really. The friend I had helping me out is simply not responding to the calls I'm making," she replied, feeling a wave of frustration wash over her.

"Do you want to use my phone?" he offered, hope tinging his tone.

"Oh, can I?" she asked, her surprise evident in her voice.

"Sure, I have international calling on my phone," he stated confidently, handing her his device with a reassuring smile.

Why had she not thought of this solution before? She raised the phone to her ear and listened as it rang through the quiet room. A couple of seconds passed, then an angry male voice broke the tension.

"Hello."

"Luke," she exclaimed in a mix of relief and surprise upon hearing his voice. "You're not answering your phone. I was worried something had happened to you."

"No, I'm fine. I just don't have any money right now. I'm not your man, Rena. Why don't you ask your man to help you instead? What happened to the church people? Can't they help you?"

She thought briefly about the troublesome and arrogant Behanzin she had left behind in Buffalo, as well as the church community that had unceremoniously put her out just a week before she secured her last job. However, she quickly pushed those thoughts out of her mind. This was the Luke Rena remembered, and this attitude was precisely why she had broken up with him all those years ago, yet had managed to remain friends. This was the very reason she could never return to him on an intimate level, the way he had always hoped she would.

"Luke, just help me this last time, I promise I will try not to bother you again," she begged, her voice tinged with desperation and shame. Not caring at all that Alphonso was right there, listening in on the conversation like an unwelcome specter.

"This is really the last time. I'm not your man. You'll have to find someone else to help you. Go find a man, Rena!" He slammed down the phone with finality, leaving a chilling silence in its wake.

He had a storage room packed to the ceiling with hundred dollar bills, rats gnawing away at the edges of his fortune. The entire globe was suffering under a severe pandemic, and he was telling her to go find a man. She didn't take a moment to dissect the potential implications of his harsh words; she was simply too relieved that she had managed to pay her mounting bills. Handing Alphonso back his phone and giving him her debit card, she quickly cleared up her overdue bills and secured the room for the week ahead. When he returned her card, she immediately headed to the supermarket to load up on essential food items, including coffee, water, Tostadas Chips, and toiletries. She was running low on toothpaste, and her body lotion was completely empty.

That night, new local guests were placed in the room right next to hers. She could hear everything they said—as if she was sharing the room with them. Through her scratching frenzy, she heard the woman spray something fragrant, and seconds later, the most beautiful perfume scent she had encountered in years seeped through the walls, tantalizing her nostrils. Rena's relentless itching suddenly ceased, and an overwhelming sense of relief washed over her. She sagged back onto the bed and drifted into a deep, peaceful sleep almost immediately.

The next morning, when she awoke, itch-free and refreshed, she checked her door and discovered the lock was indeed open, but the suitcases behind the door remained exactly where they had been left. She wandered into the bathroom, surveyed the tiled space, and came to a decision: it would become her new sleeping quarters from that moment on.

Her first night on the bathroom floor turned out to be the best sleep she had experienced during her entire stay at the hotel. The soothing quiet enveloping the bathroom sent waves of serotonin flooding through her brain, leaving her feeling pleasantly sedate and remarkably fresh. It was pure bliss. She reveled in this unexpected feeling of peace, allowing herself to drift back into slumber for a few more precious hours. Eventually, she was jolted awake by the loud slamming of the toilet seat and the unmistakable sound of the toilet flushing from the room above her. She lay there for a moment, bracing herself for the unpleasant smell of shit to assail her senses, but to her relief, nothing came. Feeling satisfied and itch-free, she decided to do some gentle stretching—the first time in quite a while. Once she completed her stretches, she felt invigorated and ready to face the day, so she made her way to the small kitchenette to brew some much-needed coffee.

Thousands of people had inexplicably gone missing in Mexico, creating a climate of fear and uncertainty. The pervasive underground prostitution networks and the sordid sales of human organs thrived as a multi-billion dollar corporation, hidden from the eyes of the law. It was the fateful night when a mysterious woman had sprayed some potent substance that had promptly put Rena to sleep, which made her suddenly and painfully aware of the very real danger she had unwittingly placed herself in.

This sobering realization made her sensitive to the precarious situation she now found herself in—a single woman, alone and vulnerable in the sprawling expanse of Mexico City, with no one to turn to for help. Overwhelmed, she sank down onto the cold, hard floor, held her head in her trembling hands, and let the tears flow freely in a much-needed release.

Once she had gathered herself and finished crying, she washed her long, tangled locks, took a long, calming shower, dressed herself, carefully dried the bathroom floor to maintain a sense of order, and then made her makeshift bed right there on it. Yes, it felt so much safer than before, and the window was conveniently located right there in the bathroom, positioned above the roof of the garage and hotel entryway.

Although the window was securely grilled up and not at all inviting for escape, birds were the only things that ever passed by, creating a small sense of life outside. As she assessed her circumstances, she felt undeniably better.

Moving into the bathroom turned out to be quite beneficial, as it did wonders for her incessantly itchy skin, alleviating her urge to scratch. However, she couldn't help but wonder why the relentless itching did not cease even after she had moved out of the other hotel. Rena found herself unable to figure out the underlying reason for her discomfort.

She speculated that her pre-diabetic condition had probably escalated into full-blown type two diabetes, prompting her to eliminate sugar and a number of unhealthy foods from her diet. Yet, she soon noticed that the itching was most pronounced when her body was deficient in moisture.

Since the air in Mexico City was famously dry, she had realized she didn't sweat here—not once. This was the only place she had ever been where she could not break a sweat, and the realization was both perplexing and disheartening.

Whenever she felt the discomfort of itching creeping in, she would seek refuge beneath the sheets, staying there until her body finally started to produce some sweat. While she occasionally attempted some light exercise, she found herself lacking the motivation to commit fully, so hiding under the sheets became her makeshift itch relief therapy. Exhausted from the day's struggles, she eventually drifted off to sleep during yet another session of her unconventional therapeutic practice.

Just as she was sinking into a deep slumber, a voice cut through the silence, whispering, "You have been ignoring me."

Her heart nearly leaped out of her chest, pounding fiercely as if trying to escape. She thought she had finally managed to get rid of him for good. Yet, here he was. The sound of his voice was doing inexplicable things to her neurons—affecting every single cell in her body with an intensity that left her breathless. The overwhelming desperation and longing she felt when he was near was threatening to completely overwhelm her senses.

"Breathe," she repeated to herself. Slowly, she inhaled deeply and exhaled deliberately. In and out, she reminded herself as she fought to regain composure. As she opened her eyes, still focusing on her steady breathing, she sought to calm herself amidst the tumult inside. He never revealed himself during her waking moments, only haunting her in her dreams; this had led her to believe she was safe for the time being. Where on earth was he now? Why had he chosen to show himself after so many long months of silence? The mere thought of him frustrated her to no end. Now, she would have to summon the strength to force herself to stay awake.

"Fuck it!" she exclaimed, determined to resist the pull of the dream world.

"THE TREES MAY NOT HAVE EYES LIKE US, BUT THEY'RE SEEING EVERYTHING, EVEN THE DUST."

"THE TREES MAY NOT HAVE MOUTH LIKE US, BUT THEY EAT, SPEAK AND NEVER MAKE FUSS."

"THE TREES MAY NOT HAVE EARS LIKE US, BUT THEY'RE LISTENING TO EVERYTHING, EVEN WHEN WE FIGHT AND CUSS."

"THE TREES MAY NOT HAVE FEET LIKE US, BUT THEY'RE WALKING, EVEN WHILE YOU CATCH THE BUS."

Chapter 9
THE TWINS

"Hey you two, you better stop, or else me a come in there!" Gean warned, her voice loud and firm, directed squarely at the two restless beings she was lovingly carrying inside her uterus. She was utterly sick and tired of them persistently trying to kick each other out of her.

In response to her call, they paused for a brief moment, eagerly waiting to see what might happen next. Their little hearts thumping rapidly at the thrilling prospect of catching a glimpse of her through the thin barrier that separated them from the outside world. Then she heard them giggle softly, perhaps at the absurdity of the idea or maybe they were courageously daring her to make a move.

"Is that so? Kick each other one more time and see," she replied, her tone playful yet serious.

The twin girls exchanged glances, wide-eyed and surprised by her words. They turned their curious eyes to the delicate membrane that stood between them and the bustling outside world. They could hardly see through it, as the proliferation of veins, amniotic liquid, and various other matters lining the membrane walls were all obstructing their tiny views. But her threat sounded undeniably serious; could she really do it? With that thought lingering in their minds, they quieted down for a moment, not wanting to provoke any further intrusion into their peaceful little sanctuary.

"Yes, go to sleep," they heard her mumble softly, her voice soothing and laced with warmth.

They looked at each other again, not daring to whisper a single peep. They clearly felt her walking with purpose to the kitchen. They heard the rhythmic sounds of her preparing breakfast, familiar and comforting. In their minds, they tasted every spoonful of food that she swallowed, longing for that experience to be theirs too. Today, it was a warm bowl of porridge accompanied by crunchy crackers, both of which were their absolute favorite. Once they were done feeding, they succumbed to sleep, wrapping their tiny arms around each other in an innocent embrace.

"About time," Gean muttered under her breath when she felt them finally quiet down. Ever since they had become aware of each other in her womb, she had not been able to enjoy a peaceful, uninterrupted sleep. The moment she closed her eyes, they would start wanting to play or fight, tumbling around as if they were already in the world. Often, she found herself gently tapping on her swollen belly to encourage them to calm down.

"The little chits! I can't wait for them to get out and explore." At eight months pregnant, Gean was so large that she could hardly walk without discomfort. Although she knew she should be resting, there was no one around to tend to her needs, forcing her to go against the doctor's orders. She carefully finished washing the porridge pan, the bowls, and last night's dishes before she methodically swept the floor.

Exhaustion crept over her like a heavy blanket, so she settled down on the small bed in her tiny studio. But her body screamed for sleep, so she laid back and closed her eyes, drifting off into a much-needed rest. Two hours later, however, the twins were at it again, wildly stirring and kicking, waking her from her brief slumber. She laid still, purposely breathing slowly and deeply, with her eyes closed as she focused her attention inward, willing her inner being to shrink down until it was the size of the babies she was carrying. Then, she found herself astral traveling into her uterus.

"How many times do I have to tell the two of you to cut it out?" she yelled exasperatedly at them.

"What, you think I was threatening you with empty

words? If you two don't behave yourselves…!" She left the thought hanging ominously in the air, hoping that they could somehow sense her seriousness.

The two were looking at her with the most ridiculous and utterly shocked look on their faces, a combination of disbelief and surprise that was almost comical. If she wasn't so tired and sleep-deprived, she would have laughed heartily at their expressions. Gean, however, had not noticed their little hearts beating faster than normal, as she was far too focused on scolding them for so rudely disturbing her much-needed sleep.

"You two better start working it out from here, because out there," she pointed to the membrane wall that was securely protecting them, "it's a bad world, and if you can't manage to live in here without fighting each other, you certainly will tear each other apart out there."

The shock at seeing her was sending their weak little hearts into what felt like cardiac arrest. Meanwhile, her body was starting to go into labor, a reality that seemed to come with its own urgency. Finally, her sleep-deprived brain began to register the alarming changes in their pallor, prompting her to astral travel back to her physical body.

The bed was bloodied, and she could feel her amniotic fluid pooling uncomfortably under her back where she lay. Why did she do that to herself? And to them? She desperately tried to calm her thundering heart, praying that they were okay and safe.

Without moving her weary body, Gean reached for the phone she kept by her pillow for emergencies just like this one. She dialed a number and waited anxiously.

"Hello. Ananuyah, help me," she managed to utter before the phone fell out of her hand, darkness enveloping her as she lost consciousness.

When Gean finally woke up, she found herself lying on a bed in The May Pen General Hospital, a place that was uncomfortably familiar as it was just a stone's throw away from her studio-flat in May Pen, Clarendon, Jamaica. She could feel the sensation of being hooked up to many tubes and monitors, each one tirelessly tracking her blood pressure, heart rate, and pulse.

"How you feeling?" came the gentle voice of her friend, Ananuyah, cutting through the haze of her thoughts.

Gean slowly turned her head toward her friend, but instead of answering her question, she immediately asked, "The baby dem awright?" Her heart raced as she waited for a response, bracing herself for the worst.

Ananuyah sighed deeply, her gaze heavy as she looked at Gean. She weighed the options in her mind, wondering if she should reveal the painful truth or offer a more generic, comforting answer—perhaps until Gean was feeling a little bit better.

"They couldn't save one of the twins, and the other one is in critical condition. You're not doing so well yourself, as you can see," she finally said, opting for honesty.

Gean averted her face from Ananuyah and squeezed her eyes shut tight, but despite her efforts, the tears spilled uncontrollably down her cheeks. It felt like a crushing weight bearing down on her; the guilt was suffocating, and she couldn't shake the thought that it was all her fault. She should have never frightened them so terribly. The guilt, so profoundly overwhelming, latched itself into her soul like a vise; it constricted around her already fragile heart, and as if to emphasize her anguish, she began to cough painfully.

Her time was drawing near, she felt it strongly in her bones. With a palpable sense of urgency, she quickly turned back to her friend.

"Her name is Olowurena, but please, just call her Rena. That's what she prefers us to call her. The other one, the one who has left us, her name was Olowulena, but we affectionately called her Lena."

"Sssh," Ananuyah whispered softly, conveying a sense of calm. "We'll discuss this later, but for now, just rest."

However, Gean was already gone, slipping away silently. In that moment, two dedicated nurses burst into the room, alarmed by the incessant beeping of the monitor. Ananuyah could only watch in disbelief as Gean walked out of the hospital room, cradling a newborn baby in her arms, her face radiating a huge, joyful smile directed down at the precious infant.

~~~~~~~

Rena woke up with a start, unsettled and anxious, as she realized she had gotten that dream again. It was a distressing, recurring dream she had been experiencing ever since she turned three years old. What did it all mean? Who exactly was Ananuyah, the mysterious figure who haunted her sleep? This particular time marked the first instance where she was able to vividly recall all the intricate details connected to the dream. Her fuzzy brain tried desperately to latch onto the fleeting memory of the pregnant woman she instinctively knew was her mother. She carried with her a worn-out picture of her, a cherished token she clung to throughout the years. This was the mother she never truly knew, yet felt an unbreakable bond with— a bond that filled her heart with longing and affection.

A tear rolled silently down her cheek, landing softly onto her sheets as she thought about the profound sadness her mother must have felt at the loss of the twin sister she hardly remembered, a loss that resonated deeply within her. She closed her eyes, hoping to escape the overwhelming emotion, yet she didn't want to go back to sleep if it meant facing that haunting dream again. Instead, she decided to do a restorative Mooji meditation before turning her attention to one of her favorite YouTube channels.

The Jamaican

"THE TREES MAY NOT HAVE EYES LIKE US, BUT THEY'RE SEEING EVERYTHING, EVEN THE DUST."

"THE TREES MAY NOT HAVE EARS LIKE US, BUT THEY'RE LISTENING TO EVERYTHING, EVEN WHEN WE FIGHT AND CUSS."

"THE TREES MAY NOT HAVE MOUTH LIKE US, BUT THEY EAT, SPIT AND NEVER MAKE FUSS."

"THE TREES MAY NOT HAVE FEET LIKE US, BUT THEY'RE WALKING, EVEN WHILE YOU CATCH THE BUS."

CHAPTER 10
A SONG TO SUN

The noise of the early morning shifted Rena's attention to the expansive sky she could see from her bathroom window. She stood up on her tiptoes to look beyond the lush green trees that framed her view.

Good, the sun still has a little ways to rise before it reaches her cozy window, she thought with a sense of relief. She stretched, extending her hands above her head, reaching as far as she could toward the ceiling. With her spine straight and head falling gently back, she stayed in that position until she counted to a hundred, savoring the sensation. After finishing her stretches, she made her way to the bedroom window to throw open the curtains.

The birds were out in full force today, energetically flying around from one neighboring tree to another. There were over a hundred different species flitting about, some she didn't recognize at all.

They performed the same delightful routine every morning in eager anticipation of the rising sun. Rena had never seen them fly away to forage for food; she later learned they didn't need to, as all their needs were perfectly taken care of by the generously providing trees surrounding her home.

She watched them settle on the highest branches, gracefully waiting. It was always a pleasure to see them gather with their friends to witness the sun rising, together in perfect harmony. Her heart was filled with happiness for them.

"*Good morning, Tuck. Good morning, Nuck. Good morning, Sarai. And good morning to all the others,*" she greeted quietly, savoring the peaceful moment.

"___,"

"*Yes, I slept exceptionally well.*"

"___,"

"*Yes, I'll take a look at it just for a brief moment.*"

They all smiled warmly and nodded their heads in agreement, sharing a moment of camaraderie.

She left her place by the window to go retrieve a fresh piece of ginger from the kitchen. She peeled it carefully, reveling in the sharp, spicy aroma, and popped it into her mouth. The intense flavor made her mouth spring water almost immediately. She quickly made her way to the bathroom sink, where she began to spit, releasing remnants of overnight staleness until she was certain her mouth was completely refreshed. Then, she began to chew on the ginger, allowing its invigorating qualities to take effect. She used her tongue to maneuver the ginger remnants over her teeth and gums, savoring its zest, and when she was satisfied, she swallowed the last bits with a sense of relief.

It was Nuck who had suggested this little routine to her when he'd seen her brushing her teeth by the window previously. She felt grateful for his input, especially since her badly receding gum-lines seemed to indicate that some gum regeneration was indeed taking place; additionally, the ginger significantly kept her breath feeling fresher, much longer.

As the sun peeked over the trees, Rena's heart gladdened at the breathtaking sight before her.

"Oh my beautiful, beautiful Sun. Welcome! You are truly the most amazing phenomenon my eyes have ever beheld. I want to gaze upon your wondrous beauty all day long. I wish to compose poetry and sing melodious songs about your surreal splendor to the world and even beyond."

Rena looked intently into the sun rising gracefully above the trees. She had never witnessed anything quite so astounding, and every single morning, she looked into the sun, experiencing the same profound amazement that took her breath away anew each day.

"As the Earth gracefully twirled her azure beauty around you, you continued to generously give her your radiant brilliance, though it was only a fraction of what you truly possessed. Your intense heat and your shining glory were gifts that we all profoundly recognized and cherished. You tirelessly kept the Earth beautiful and vibrant with your warmth, making it possible for me to rise each day and joyfully embrace you upon my feet. Each morning, I eagerly look forward to witnessing your magnificent ascent. My beautiful Sun, thank you for yesterday's glow, thank you for today's light, and thank you for tomorrow's promise too."

Rena gazed at the blue sun rotating slowly, reminiscent of a disk in a CD player. Today, it was surrounded by a gentle white light, reflecting her inner balance and harmony. She was not afraid today, and her eyes were free from the stress that typically accompanied her gaze into the sun's brilliance.

There were times when she would sleep on her eyes, only to be awaken with a sense of distress. The pain would get worst when she look into the sun's brilliance, resulting in the aura of red, or orange around. Overtime, she learned that the shifting colors of the sun's aura were a manifestation of the various emotions she was feeling in that moment.

"My beautiful Sun, words fail to fully capture the stunning beauty you reflect upon us. Could you kindly warm my scalp for me? Thank you."

She had discovered, during quarantine, that asking the sun to warm her scalp was a vastly different experience from simply walking in its light. It allowed her to connect on a deeper level with its warmth.

She gently took off the scarf that she had tied around her head before bed, carefully unraveling its grip. Her beautiful locks unfolded and cascaded down until they fell gracefully to her bottom, creating a shimmering curtain. With delicate movements, she parted her hair down the middle and bowed her head to the bright sun, allowing its warm rays to penetrate and soothe her scalp. She counted slowly to twenty, savoring the sensation, then raised her head to the sun once more, this time keeping her eyes closed tightly, focusing intently on the comforting heat enveloping her face. Again, she counted to twenty, feeling at one with the moment. Turning her back to the sun, she elevated her head slightly so that its light could reach her seventh chakra—an essential energy point located at the very top of her head that she had been born with. With deep concentration, she counted to twenty again. She then bent her head forward so the sun could connect with the lower half of her head, zeroing in on the area where her cerebellum resided. When she sensed the sunlight merging with her energy, she counted steadily to twenty, feeling the warmth seep into her being.

Finishing her sun relaxation and nourishing vitamin D treatment, she turned to face the brilliance of the sun once more.

"Thank you, my brilliant, perfect Sun. Thank you for your warmth, your energy, and your power. Thank you for shinning down on us all. Without you we would not be here, so I thank you for everything. I'll see you later."

Rena tried not to think of how silly and childish she may sound, talking to the Sun in her mind. But it brought her immense happiness, so why should she care what others thought?

She glanced around at her friends, yet was unable to see them clearly. Blinking hard, she noticed that only shadows penetrated her sight, dim silhouettes against the brightness. She had learned long ago that when the sun was positioned above them in such a way, it cast their figures into a black and unrecognizable state.

With a smile and a wave to them, knowing they were watching her, she resumed her ritual of massaging around her eyes with a splash of vinegar to stimulate tears—another practiced habit she had developed during her sun-gazing journey.

It was yet another wind-free morning, graced with a beautiful, clear blue sky above. It was still too early to tell if rain would grace them later, but she knew she would have to wait until the sun shifted over her friends to uncover the answers.

Rena went about making herself a comforting cup of her special coffee brew, savoring each moment of the ritual. She had been cherishing one particularly delightful ingredient for the past two weeks, sometimes recycling it for two to three days before finally throwing it out. This flavorful ingredient was as fresh as it could be on the first day, and she planned to enjoy it alongside some crisp tortillas that complemented her morning perfectly.

"Hello, hello, hello," Matilda greeted loudly from downstairs, her voice echoing through the air.

Rena immediately became alert, but soon relaxed, knowing that "hello" meant a child had entered the premises and would be perfectly safe. She chuckled softly to herself, finding amusement in the notion that it was always a bit of fun listening to the cat communicating in a way that resembled human speech.

"Thanks, Matilda," she said under her breath, gently sending her gratitude on the wind from her lips to the cat's attentive ears. After she finished preparing her breakfast, Rena decided to take her meal to the bathroom, where she could enjoy her food in peace. She turned on her phone, navigating to YouTube to watch Trent and Allie—her favorite couple who shared their adventures online. They were in the process of building their dream house on sprawling acres of land, and Rena couldn't help but live vicariously through their inspiring journey, filling her mind with their dreams.

She tried not to dwell too much on her own future, as it often felt obscured by the bleakness that seemed to surround her. Munching loudly on her tortilla chips and savoring her rich coffee, Rena was momentarily lost in this quiet moment of solitude when she suddenly noticed someone sitting on the bathroom seat she had covered with a towel. It was a familiar-looking woman, elegantly dressed, looking remarkably out of place in that setting, invoking a swirl of curiosity and intrigue in Rena's mind.

"Hi," Rena said, blinking in confusion as she tried to process the unexpected presence of another. But the female only sat there, her gaze fixed on Rena, looking at her with an intensity that felt both familiar and bizarre.

What's going on? Rena wondered anxiously. Why is she looking at me like that, as if I hold some deep secret?

Her spiraling thoughts were abruptly interrupted when the female finally spoke. "Hi," her voice infused with warmth and a twinkle in her eyes, followed by a smile that lit up her entire face, radiating a sense of relief that made Rena's heart race a little.

"What's going on?" Rena asked, her voice louder than she intended, echoing slightly in the seemingly still air. This was the first time in her waking moments that she had ever experienced such an intimate visitation. Typically, these encounters were reserved for the realms of her dreams.

"Have we met before?" she ventured, curiosity bubbling to the surface.

"Yes. Many times," the female replied with an enigmatic smile.

"I vaguely remember you, but from where?" Rena pressed, her mind desperately searching her past for any clues.

"We met at the hospital at your birth. I took you to your aunty, where you were raised," the female disclosed.

"But have we met after that?" Rena insisted, longing for more answers.

"Only in dreams," the woman replied softly, her voice carrying a weight that left Rena pondering the depths of their connection.

That certainly answered the question that had been plaguing Rena's mind. With a thoughtful nod, she recalled the last dream she had of her mother, an enigmatic figure in her dreams. The woman who appeared to her was Ananuyah.

The ethereal being smiled broadly, a warmth in her gaze, and shook her head gently as if to affirm her identity.

"Yes, I am Ananuyah."

"Am I going to die?" Rena suddenly blurted out, her mind racing as she wondered why this elegantly dressed female figure was inexplicably sitting in her bathroom.

Ananuyah's laughter tinkled like the ringing of a delicate bell, and she shook her head with kindness.

"No, you're not going to die. I just wanted to meet you."

"Okayy!" Rena exclaimed, raising her eyebrows as if to silently question, "So we have met, now what?" But instead, she found herself pondering over the mother she had never truly been able to know or understand and was filled with curiosity about what kind of person she was. This was the perfect opportunity for her to gain the insights she had always desired. She opened her mouth, ready to voice her questions, but Ananuyah swiftly raised her hand to quiet her.

"We will talk about that another time. For now, I just want to know how you're doing?"

"Well, as you can see, I'm doing quite well," Rena replied with a flourish, holding out her hand and gesturing grandly to the surroundings of her modest bathroom.

Ananuyah glanced around, shaking her head slowly. "Yes, it could be worse."

The atmosphere shifted as Ananuyah's expression became serious. "Be careful. You must be very careful."

Rena's heart skipped a beat at this grave warning. This was the second caution she was receiving from a non-material being. What on earth was going on?

"What the f…" she began to mumble, but before she could finish her thought, Ananuyah vanished, slipping away like mist in the wind, leaving Rena alone once more in the tranquility of her bathroom with riotous thoughts running through her mind.

Rena finished her breakfast, feeling perplexed and somewhat unsettled, then embarked on the quiet journey of teaching herself Spanish. She was determined to keep her newfound skill a secret, not wanting anyone to know that she was proficient at speaking the language. Furthermore, immersing herself in the intricacies of this beautiful language served as a comforting distraction, one that was genuinely helping to maintain her sanity amidst the chaos of her thoughts.

"THE TREES MAY NOT HAVE EYES LIKE US, BUT THEY'RE SEEING EVERYTHING, EVEN THE DUST."

"THE TREES MAY NOT HAVE EARS LIKE US, BUT THEY'RE LISTENING TO EVERYTHING, EVEN WHEN WE FIGHT AND CUSS."

"THE TREES MAY NOT HAVE MOUTH LIKE US, BUT THEY EAT, SPEAK AND NEVER MAKE FUSS."

"THE TREES MAY NOT HAVE FEET LIKE US, BUT THEY'RE WALKING, EVEN WHILE YOU CATCH THE BUS."

Chapter 11
THE BEATING OF THE PLASTIC DRUM

Energized from her special brew and feeling particularly confident about her Spanish skills, Rena decided that today was an auspicious day for tackling her laundry. She genuinely needed this activity to distract her from the lingering warnings that haunted her thoughts, along with the frustrating image of that cock-sucking Behanzin, who had become an unwelcome presence in her mind ever since her steamy encounter with Gerard.

Rena had long since run out of clean clothes and was currently resorting to wrapping her scarf around her hips, while wearing a sports bra accompanied by a thin sheer shirt draping over it. Though she tried to convince herself that she could stretch it out for a few more days without washing, she realized she might as well get the chore over with today.

The heat was already intense, but surprisingly, Nuck was not preoccupied with the sweltering weather today. Instead, all eyes seemed to be drawn to her window. Sheel, the sparrow, was cursing loudly at her mate, who responded only with short, clipped tweets. Rena couldn't help but laugh; the cussing sparrow had become her latest source of amusement. Loud and obnoxious, she was a true character. If Rena listened closely enough, she could almost decipher the words the furious female bird was angrily tweeting at her mate. However, the male sparrow was evidently wise, opting to keep his retorts minimal today.

Yesterday, though, was an entirely different scenario. The two of them had engaged in such a loud argument that they almost shattered the tranquil quiet of the outside world. The trees and other birds remained silent, not daring to breathe amidst the fury pouring from Sheel. Rena listened intently, bracing herself for a potential fight, but to her surprise, all the sparrows did was trade curses back and forth.

Without thinking twice, she stood up and swiftly switched the YouTube channel to Luciano Pavarotti, her absolute favorite opera singer, who was the only one capable of helping her through a long day filled with the dreaded task of doing laundry by hand.

Living in the cramped quarters of Mexico City taught her invaluable lessons in being spatially savvy.

Here, in the small bathroom, there was frustratingly nowhere to hang her freshly washed clothing. The shower area was cut off by a wall, featuring only a modest opening for the door. Meanwhile, the water closet and wash sink shared the limited thirty-six square feet of space, which allowed her to creatively utilize the remaining area for her personal needs.

With no available wall space to set up a proper clothesline, she ingeniously suspended her garments on sturdy clothes hangers, securing them in place with bright color clothes pins. Thanks to the separation of the shower area from the rest of the bathroom, she was fortunate enough to have two towel holders to serve dual purposes for her hangers.

She washed and carefully hung her clothing up to drip dry, all the while belting out off-key notes to Pavarotti's stirring melodies, blissfully indifferent to the fact that she was still in a hotel room.

Occasionally, the unpleasant memory of that cocky Behanzin threatened to invade her thoughts, but that was precisely when she sang the loudest, hoping the noise would drown him out and banish him from her mind for good.

Sometimes she would look through the bathroom window at her friends, only to find them trying to catch a glimpse of her, as well. After finishing with her laundry nearly two hours later, with her hands now shriveled from the prolonged exposure to water, she decided to seek out Maria, one of the diligent cleaning maids working at the hotel.

"Buenos dias, Maria. Do you have towels?" she asked, spotting the maid busily working in room 2021B down the hallway.

"Tienes todos?" Maria inquired, fully aware that Rena's grasp of Spanish was quite limited. Rena knew she needed not only fresh sheets but also other essential hotel necessities that typically accompanied a clean room.

"Si, todos. Gracias," she replied gratefully. As Maria went to fetch her requested items, Rena took the initiative to strip the bed of its top layer, gathering all the dirty sheets and towels, which she then neatly placed in front of the door for easy collection.

Spotting the broom Maria had leaned against the door opposite hers, she picked it up and began sweeping the dark red commercial carpeted floor, making it look presentable. When she finished sweeping, she selected the cleanest towel from the dirty pile and proceeded to wipe away the dust that had settled on the mirrors and other surfaces throughout the room.

Just then, Maria returned, carrying a stack of bed sheets, fresh towels, two small bottles of water, and a small package containing an assortment of shampoos and miniature bathing soaps. Though none of these were actually used, Rena noticed that the collection of shampoos and soaps was steadily piling up in a container on a shelf in the bathroom, untouched and gathering dust.

"Muchísimo gracias, Maria," Rena expressed warmly to the kind maid, gratefully accepting the substantial load that Maria had been carrying in her hands. She carefully placed the items on the bed, then reached for her own pile of dirty laundry and handed it over to Maria without hesitation.

It always amazed her that the hotel maids here did not seem to get repulsed by her when they took her soiled sheets. Even during the Covid-19 pandemic, a time when many individuals were understandably wary of any form of contact, they always treated her with the same kindness and respect as they had before. Rena felt a deep sense of gratitude for that unwavering compassion. She often wished she could offer the kind maids something in return for their kindness.

One day, she promised herself, future Rena would be in a position to give back to this lovely, hardworking staff.

~~~~~

She meticulously made the bed with the top covers, leaving the remaining bedding for the bathroom transitioning later on. As she dug through the pile of clean clothing she had left, she finally unearthed an old pair of comfy shorts and a brightly colored scarf that reminded her of summer days. Eager to freshen up, she headed to the bathroom to wash her hair and enjoy a revitalizing shower. After cleansing herself, she took her time oiling her skin and then blow drying her hair.

Rena felt a surge of happiness as she reveled in the fact that it was a delightfully hot day. To her relief, she noticed she hadn't itched even once, and she quietly wished it could stay like this for the entire duration of her stay.

The bathroom remained damp from the dripping clothes, prompting her to seek refuge on the bed. Feeling quite fatigued, she decided that a little rest would do her some much-needed good. Overall, it turned out to be a surprisingly good day, and the satisfaction of having washed her clothes lifted her spirits even more. Clad in the scarf wrapped snugly around her bust and the airy shorts, she looked ready for a beach outing; however, the reality was that there was no beach for her to enjoy.

She approached the window, waved to her very curious friends, and then gently closed the curtains to block out the world outside. Exhaustion draped over her like a heavy blanket. She spread one of the hotel sheets over the bed, then positioned a towel where her head would rest, meticulously protecting her still damp hair from touching the bed linens. The gentle breeze from the fan, paired with the towel, would finish the job of drying her thick hair.

    She climbed into bed, her entire body aching with discomfort. The pain was a harsh reminder of the long hours she had spent lying uncomfortably on the floor and the lack of any physical activity.

    The soft comfort of the bed felt heavenly, and she snuggled into the warm blankets, ready to indulge in a much-needed afternoon nap. She closed her eyes tightly, attempting to give in to the alluring embrace of sleep, but no rest came immediately. Suddenly, the inky blackness behind her eyelids transformed into a brilliant white light that gradually faded away to reveal a stunning purple sky framed by dark, imposing mountains. She blinked in disbelief, and just like that, the enchanting scene vanished. Rena waited, holding her breath, focusing intensely on the flickering light. To her astonishment, it emerged once more, and she found herself gazing up at the mesmerizing purple sky and the shadowy mountains. She couldn't help but wonder if she was truly looking up at the Kingdom of God.

    "The Kingdom of God is within you," she recalled from *Luke 17:21*.

Is this really the Kingdom of God? she pondered quietly to herself. However, each time she blinked, the stunning imagery slipped away. Sometimes the sky appeared light blue, a hopeful hue, but more often, it showcased deep shades of blue or rich purple.

The thought of being in the Kingdom of God filled her with a sense of peace. Did this mean she would need to be dead first to experience it? The very idea of being dead, oddly enough, didn't seem so daunting. She would no longer have to worry about hotel bills, the daily struggle for food, or the never-ending concerns about money—those worries would vanish forever.

As this comforting thought wrapped around her mind, she felt an unexpected sense of tranquility regarding her potential entrance into the Kingdom of God. With that hopeful notion lingering in her thoughts, she finally drifted off to sleep.

~~~~~~

"Bang, bang, bang!!!"

The loud, jarring sound of a plastic bucket being beaten relentlessly with a wooden baton suddenly startled her awake from her restless slumber. A pounding headache quickly ensued, spinning through her thoughts like a whirlwind. She held on to her head as if to prevent her brain from flying out. The overwhelming headache caused her body to shake.

Something, she couldn't comprehend, was happening to her as she continue to tremble from the accumulated stress that the unexpected and intrusive noise had arouse.

It sounded as if the raucous clattering was emanating from the next room over. Slowly, with head in her hands she reluctantly got out of bed towards the direction the sound was coming from, but it did not return.

It was now the end of her sixth week in the hotel, a place that had become all too familiar, yet increasingly unsettling. The beating of the bucket drum had started on the very first day of her fourth week. The initial time she had heard it, it was in the dead of midnight, leaving her startled and confused. She had thought something alarming was happening downstairs, perhaps some sort of commotion. She sat up in bed, anxiously waiting for the sound of music to follow the drumbeat, but it never came. Only an oppressive silence filled the room. Turning on her side, she attempted to go back to sleep. Yet as soon as she began to drift off again, the chaotic beating of the bucket erupted once more.

Long ago, during her childhood growing up in Clarendon, Jamaica they would beat an iron pot with a metal spoon over the heads of their chickens or hens if they were being attacked, hoping to save them from certain doom. The loud and vigorous beating would often revive those dazed creatures, making them get up and run away in a frantic escape. But she reminded herself fiercely that she was not a chicken, and this was a hotel, regardless of the unfortunate fact that she was late with her payment.

The relentless noise continued throughout the night, every hour, on the hour, mercilessly disrupting her peace. She was left a shaking wreck the following morning after the first night it happened. The maddening sound persisted in its torment for the next five days and nights, each instance reinforcing her mounting anxiety. She couldn't help but feel that someone was purposely trying to drive her away. But who in the world would do something so cruel? And why? There were so many empty rooms in the hotel. Who would want her gone so desperately that they would create such a cacophony just to disturb her?

Because she owed the hotel a significant amount of money, she didn't want to go and complain to Alphonso, fearing that it might complicate things further. Rena reluctantly got up and looked around for hidden cameras—struggling to control the growing sense of paranoia that threatened to overwhelm her—and couldn't find any signs of them. The noise always began the very moment she closed her eyes, echoing ominously in the stillness. Whether it was coming from the bed beneath her or from the bathroom nearby, it felt like a constant intrusion. Were they watching her sleep so they could make annoying noises just to torment her? Did they want to drive her to the point of getting fed up and leaving? Did they even know she was trying to sleep? But how on earth would they know?

CHAPTER 12
THE WATCHERS

She went into the bathroom and stood firmly before the mirror, gazing intently at her stress-ridden face that reflected her current state of anxiety. The unpleasant and lingering smell of an unwashed body wafted to her nostrils, prompting her to wrinkle up her nose in distaste. Leaning over to press her nose against the cold windowpane, she was hoping for the same scent to assault her nostrils, but only fresh air of the outdoors caressed her face. Reluctantly, she returned to stand before the mirror once more. This time, she truly focused on her reflection.

As her eyes wandered, she noticed the flickering image of the streetlight through the glass and suddenly spotted a camera aimed directly at her window from the streetlight post. Rena's heart raced with shock. Just then, a vivid scene from a chilling movie she had watched years ago surged back into her mind. She recalled the tense moment when the protagonist had been brushing her teeth in the mirror, dressed only in her undergarments, while her obsessive stalker lurked in the room opposite, fixated on her through the very same glass.

A camera and a stalker? But why was this happening to her? Rena was not always the quickest thinker, but once she began to process a situation, she invariably arrived at the right conclusions.

Without wasting another second, she hurried to her neatly organized suitcases. Digging fervently through one, her fingers brushed against the stunning, shocking color pink headscarf she had planned to use to style her hair. Grabbing it along with a roll of two-sided tape she had purchased nearly a year ago but had never utilized, she took decisive action. She carefully placed the tape on the tiles surrounding the mirror, then skillfully affixed the scarf onto the adhesive tape, ensuring it stayed in place.

A deep sense of relief washed over her, and she gave a small, almost imperceptible nod of her head. Quietly, she slipped back into the room and carefully snuck under the covers of the bed, determined to find solace in sleep once again. Holding her breath in anticipation, she listened intently for the dreaded sound of the beating bucket to echo again. When that distressing noise didn't manifest, her relief was nothing short of profound.

As she began to doze off once more, another unsettling sound abruptly intruded upon her fragile sleep. It was the unmistakable noise of furniture being dragged, scraping loudly against the floor, drowning out the faint sound of a child moaning somewhere nearby. The sounds were emerging from the room directly above her, piercing through the quiet of the day. It was not the first time she had been awakened by this child's agonizing cries. The child seemed to be suffering from an acute form of autism, his repetitive moaning resembling the sounds often made by children with that condition. She could only imagine the child's face, with drool running down both corners of his mouth in distress. Perhaps he was rocking back and forth, as many autistic children are known to do, seeking comfort in rhythm.

Rena initially tried to dismiss the noise, but then the occupant above her resumed scraping his chair across the flooring with an infuriatingly persistent motion. Was the furniture noise now serving as a disturbing substitute for the earlier beating plastic drum? She fought to resist the pull of sleep, realizing that the sudden cacophony was playing tricks on her mind. She listened intently, her thoughts intertwined with the moaning child and the incessant movement of the rolling chair across the floor, creating a haunting symphony of anxiety that kept her firmly awake.

Shouldn't the floor be carpeted? Why was the unsettling noise coming to her so loudly and suddenly? She was focused now, fully engaged in the moment. As she concentrated, she realized with a pang of concern that the child didn't sound autistic at all. Instead, it seemed as though he was gagged and tied up, struggling to make himself heard. He sounded truly stressed and distressed. The louder he moaned, the more pronounced the scraping of the chair on the floor became, creating a dreadful cacophony.

Rena had always wondered why the hotel wasn't getting the occupancy it truly deserved. The prices were significantly better than some of the hostels and hotels in Mexico City. The rooms were notably larger and far cleaner. Additionally, every room had its own private bathroom, eliminating the need for sharing with anyone else.

She vividly remembered almost catching Covid-19 at the Zocala Hostel from sharing a bathroom and various amenities with strangers. She also recalled the dreaded bed bugs, instilling a deep fear within her of them getting trapped in her locks and wreaking havoc. Those dreadful bed bugs had been the final catalyst that had driven her away to The Hotel Catalina, seeking refuge and cleanliness.

There were numerous tourists in the hostels, many of whom were coughing and vomiting, making it a rather unappealing atmosphere. In stark contrast, this hotel was not only cheaper, but also offered larger rooms that were impeccably clean, complete with maid services. Why wasn't it packed to capacity? Rena decided it was time to do some thorough research on her phone about the hotel she was currently staying at.

The instant she typed in "The Universales," her phone suddenly became overheated, making it almost impossible to hold onto comfortably. That had started to happen with alarming frequency lately. She then turned on her computer to conduct her research, but as soon as she typed in the hotel's name, the computer inexplicably shut down. Finding this a little peculiar, she decided to wait about ten minutes before attempting to power up the computer again.

Using the hotel's internet was clearly not good for her devices. They always seemed to overheat or shut down entirely. Frustrated, she finally gave up and turned off all her devices after she carefully unplugged them from the hotel internet.

But she was not one to simply give up without making a genuine effort to understand the situation. She lay there, her mind racing while listening to the unsettling moaning of the child and the erratic noise coming from the old chair nearby. The incessant moving of the furniture had finally ceased—perhaps the person responsible had grown weary of the charade.

As she pondered her surroundings, she couldn't help but question why her phone had remained untouched and functional while streaming YouTube. Intrigued, she knew she had never experienced any overheating issues when watching her favorite videos.

Determined to uncover the truth, she tried once again, only to discover that numerous international guests found the hotel environment to be overwhelmingly loud and disruptive. Some described the jarring, dissonant sounds akin to the strident beating of metal against metal, while others vividly recounted the heart-wrenching cries of children piercing through the silence in the dead of night.

A few reviewers went so far as to mention the offensive banging against the walls and the disturbing, sultry screams that invaded their much-needed sleep. Most of these reviewers seemed convinced that the cacophony was not just random noise, but rather intentional and deeply troubling.

As her thoughts spiraled, she began to connect the dots, drawing a chilling conclusion about child prostitution. But then again, the hotel manager didn't seem like the type to engage in such vile activities.

Alphonso had that gentle demeanor, one that made her believe he couldn't even harm a fly. No! She forcefully shook that dark thought from her mind, desperately searching for a different explanation. But the grim reality remained—child prostitution was a thriving underground industry, especially in this part of Mexico.

Someone had undoubtedly devised a nefarious plan to exploit the hotel's very structure to their advantage. She felt a growing certainty in her gut, knowing something sinister was unfolding around her.

For three long days, she endured the relentless moaning of the boy; it was glaringly apparent to her that it was indeed a male child in distress. As her fatigue mounted from the severe lack of sleep, she finally resolved to give it a try while keeping her eyes open—after all, she had occasionally been known for attempting such a thing.

With her eyes wide open in a surreal state, she gradually fell asleep, her consciousness detaching from her physical form. In this ethereal state, she floated effortlessly through the ceiling, ascending to the room directly above her.

Within that dimly lit space, she was confronted by a heart-wrenching scene: the small child, whom she had believed to be on the autism spectrum, was actually a vulnerable boy with Down syndrome. He was tied up, completely naked against the cold wall, his mouth cruelly taped shut as he emitted muffled moans of distress.

Rena scanned the room, noting a computer desk cluttered with two laptops, an array of five iPhones, and three Samsung phones. Suddenly, one of the iPhones emitted a beep, revealing a text message written in Chinese characters across the screen. The occupant of the room was occupying the bathroom at that moment.

Just as Rena ventured inside, she caught sight of an Asian man laboriously pushing an ottoman across the slick bathroom floor, making a racket that would have certainly given her a splitting headache had she been in her physical body. She observed the short, stocky man, whose eyes glimmered with a burning hatred, as he strode back to the computer desk to respond to the text message he had just received.

Almost immediately, another Samsung phone beeped, and her heart raced as she recognized that it alerted him to an email bearing her name. He picked up the phone and began poring over her emails, his expression revealing a sinister curiosity as he discovered a message from her friend, Kimmy, who had sent her another forty dollars. Rena felt a surge of fear wash over her as she watched the pedophilic hacker scroll through her personal emails on his Samsung phone, a fear her physical being remained

The Jamaican

blissfully unaware of during this disconcerting encounter.

He clicked on one of the laptops, and it instantly came to life with a soft whir. The desktop was intriguingly split into four distinct sections, one of which was conspicuously blocked out, displaying the name of her computer—Calzadauno12—written in delicate, small letters just above it. This section was blocked out because she had her computer turned off, adding an air of mystery to the situation. The second quarter of his computer screen displayed Alphonso in his room, engaged in a lively Zoom chat with another person. He was laughing heartily, completely unaware that he was being monitored. The remaining quarter of the screen flipped disconcertingly between different cameras, providing glimpses inside various hotel rooms, revealing the intimacy and chaos of each space.

Suddenly, there was a knock, knock! The Pedophilia Hacker rose to open the door. A hotel maid, someone she had seen a few times but never had the chance to speak with, walked in. Her short, black, shiny, curly hair appeared freshly washed, confirming she had probably just started her shift. She approached the boy, swiftly untied him, and pulled out clothing and sneakers from a black plastic bag she carried in her hand. With purpose, she opened a bottle of water and took out a pill from a small container, also from the plastic bag. After carefully removing the tape from his mouth, she forced it open and hurriedly chugged the pill down his throat. The boy reacted instinctively, coughing up the pill almost immediately. Undeterred, she tried again, this time gentler and more patient, putting the water bottle to his mouth as she watched him drink eagerly, as if he hadn't had anything to drink in days.

Rena watched intently as the maid led the boy out into the dimly lit corridor, while the Pedophilia Hacker quietly closed the door behind them. All of this transpired with not a single word spoken, creating an unsettling silence that hung heavily in the air.

Pedophilia Hacker made his way back to the bathroom, pushing the ottoman across the bathroom floor with an audible scrape, before he settled himself in the office chair where he sat down with a grim sense of satisfaction.

The sound of a raven's loud crowing unexpectedly sent her spiraling through the floor back to her physical body. Ignoring the excruciating headache that throbbed insistently in her temples, she hastily grabbed the small amount of trash she had accumulated and sprinted out of the cramped room toward the staircase on her floor, where the trash disposals were inconveniently kept.

As she hurried down, she noticed the maid struggling as she dragged the little boy down the stairs to the lobby. Rena watched helplessly as the little boy dragged his tiny feet and stumbled a few times along the way, looking lost and forlorn. Tears began to stream silently down her cheeks, leaving a trail of sorrow.

She made her way back to her room, feeling strangely disoriented in her head as the headache intensified. In an effort to calm herself, she brewed a simple cup of plain coffee and took it with her to the bathroom. Sitting down on the cool tile floor, she took slow sips, desperately trying not to think about anything at all. She closed her eyes and leaned her head against the cool surface, focusing on her breathing as the relentless ache of the headache gradually began to ebb away.

It was well after six in the evening, and a sudden, profound quiet had settled over the entire hotel. Rena could sense a calming energy emanating from downstairs, wrapping around her like a comforting blanket, allowing her to finally fall asleep more peacefully than she had thought possible.

That unforgettable day when Rena slept with her eyes wide open was the very first time she experienced astral travel while her eyes remained wide open during her sleep. In the past, she had always believed she was merely dreaming when these extraordinary traveling experiences occurred, but she finally proved to herself that all along she was indeed having a genuine experience—a true out-of-body experience that was far more significant than she had ever realized. Until that moment, she had been blissfully unaware of the nature of her encounters. Unfortunately, no one was present in her life to explain these phenomena to her. For years, she had mistakenly thought she had just conjured up these bizarre experiences in her mind, ever since she turned three years old. Almost every single night, she had inexplicably left her physical body, regardless of whether her eyes were opened or closed, to embark on her astral adventures, always returning just in time for the morning when it was time to awaken. Later that very evening, when she checked her phone, she discovered an unexpected email—Kimmy, her dear American friend, had generously sent her another forty dollars. It was also that same night when Matilda arrived at the hotel, where she began channeling the mysterious cat.

The Jamaican

Chapter 13
HUNGER MANAGEMENT

❝Rena, my friend wants to sample your pussy," Behanzin, her boyfriend, said to her, breaking the silence that had settled over them.

She felt an overwhelming wave of shock wash over her at his unexpected words. How could she possibly respond to such an outrageous proposition? What had given him the impression that she would be into something so risqué? Did she inadvertently convey any signals that hinted at her being that kind of adventurous?

Rena couldn't shake the thought as she recalled her last ten years spent in the church, where she had cultivated a sense of purity and restraint. When she finally chose to be intimate with him, she felt like a new virgin navigating uncharted waters. The mere idea that he would think she would consider being with his friend seemed utterly ridiculous.

Her mind raced as she thought about the friend he was mentioning—a man who was anything but appealing, one of the oldest pimps she had ever encountered. He was a shallow old veteran who prided himself on believing he was God's gift to women, often boasting that no woman could resist his charm. But Rena had never shown him a flicker of interest. He was simply not her type, and she could sense his resentment toward her because of her self-assured nature. To him, every woman was merely a conquest.

"You want to push my pussy onto your friend? Are you tired of me already?" she retorted, trying to mask her disbelief with indignation.

"No," he replied hastily, "I owe him money. He said he would cancel my debt if he could have sex with you."

"So you're pimping me out now? You want to turn me into a prostitute?" Rena's voice trembled with disbelief and outrage. She couldn't fathom being caught in such an absurd situation. She had genuinely thought she was developing a meaningful relationship with a person who was decent and respectful. He certainly had acted that way, at least until this shocking moment.

"It's only this one time, Rena," Behanzin insisted, his tone alarmingly casual, as if this bizarre request was a common, everyday occurrence in his life.

Just then, her Soulmate chose that precise moment to assert itself—a rare manifestation during her waking hours. The anger she had been striving to stifle suddenly erupted from him like a tidal wave.

"I think it's time for me to go," she stated firmly to both of them, hoping to regain control of the situation.

"You're not going anywhere!" Behanzin shouted angrily, snatching her by the neck with his huge, calloused right hand while hastily unzipping his pants with the other. His demeanor was now that of a complete stranger, someone she could hardly recognize.

Before she could process her next thought, he was hurled violently across the room, crashing into the wooden wall with a resounding thud.

Rena didn't spare a moment to witness the shock etched on his face; driven by an overwhelming need to escape, she bolted out the door into the uncertain night beyond.

Trying to put the overwhelming feeling of madness as far away from her as possible, she had taken the bus to the movie theatre located on Main Street in Buffalo. There, she remained for a disorienting five hours, not actually watching any films, but instead engrossed in making plans for her next calculated move. She had made a grave mistake in her life, a choice which she was now paying dearly for with the weight of regret.

Rena knocked her chest gently, attempting to rid herself of the persistent pain that had lodged itself deep within her heart. Quiet tears rolled down her cheeks as she desperately tried to ignore the ominous presence sitting nearby, unsure of what she should do next.

That night, when she returned to Kensington Avenue, back to the apartment she had rented from him, she was met with yet another shocking revelation. Behanzin was lying carelessly in her bed with the very man he had intended to pimp her out to. Although she shouldn't have been surprised, she had felt an inclination toward this situation all along, yet she had chosen to ignore it.

In a sudden rush of emotions, she quickly closed the door behind her and left without looking back, opting instead to spend the night in the solitude of an Airbnb.

~~~~~~

She rolled over on her makeshift bed, situated on the bathroom floor, listening intently to the low, muttered voices coming from the rooms that were further away from hers. Keeping her eyes tightly shut, she tried to ignore their chatter. She knew she should get up and go socialize with her friends, but she really wasn't in the mood to face the world just yet. Instead, she rolled again, savoring the temporary comfort of her bed and the blissful quietness enveloping her. Although part of her recognized that she really should get up and go talk to her friends, another part of her simply didn't want to.

Rena realized what this peculiar feeling was. The time spent in the hotel had taught her that she shouldn't allow herself to feel relaxed. That she shouldn't truly enjoy the fleeting moment. This sense of peace had been elusive since moving in, and the one time it seemed that she was finally going to have a good day, it felt like she was already sabotaging it.

She rolled onto her back with a heavy sigh, glancing up at the ceiling, and wondered where Pedophilia Hacker had gone. It struck her as odd that she hadn't heard him in several days. She stared at the tiled ceiling and tried to imagine him up there, lifeless and gone. Shaking the wicked thoughts from her mind, she still wished wherever he was, he would remain there.

Deciding to stop torturing herself with these dark musings, she turned onto her side, choosing to take full advantage of the peaceful moment that was so rare. Closing her eyes, she sighed blissfully before succumbing to sleep, hoping that maybe this time, she could find a little respite from her worries.

Suddenly, she jolted awake with a start. There was a loud, relentless pounding on her door that sliced through the tranquility and instantly gave her a throbbing headache. Without a moment to spare, she hurriedly left the cramped bathroom to open the door. To her surprise, Maria stood there, looking more anxious than usual. The woman thrust her phone at Rena with a measure of aggression, her eyes wide with urgency.

"They need their money for the room," she snapped, clearly frustrated. Rena realized she hadn't paid them in over eight long days. She reluctantly took the phone and glanced at the message displayed on the screen.

"Can you go downstairs to the office?" it read, sending a new wave of dread coursing through her.

Rena handed the young woman back her phone with a subtle nod of her head, wishing to convey understanding amidst the tension.

"Dos minutos," she told her firmly, holding up two fingers to emphasize the urgency of the situation.

Maria, however, shook her head in frustration before walking off, leaving Rena feeling an overwhelming sense of dread. The inevitable had come knocking with relentless persistence. It was time for her to prepare herself to face the streets, to navigate a world much like the other homeless individuals who had been forced to abandon their dreams and comforts.

Her heart raced, beating faster than it ever had before. To slow it down, she focused intently on Maria's brusque attitude, reminding herself that the two women had, in fact, treated her quite well in the past. However, they also bore the heavy burden of needing to care for their own families during this challenging crisis. If there were no guests, they simply could not earn a living. Rena understood this harsh reality and did her best not to take Maria's demeanor too personal.

With hesitant movements, Rena dragged on a long, hated dress that she rarely wore, paired with simple slippers, feeling the fabric cling uncomfortably to her skin. Her pounding heart only intensified the throbbing headache that had taken residence within her. She tried to take deep, calming breaths, hoping that more oxygen would help ease her pain, but the relief she sought was nowhere to be found. Instead, with every step she took, her heart seemed to race even faster, escalating her panic attack and further fueling her already unbearable headache.

The lingering thought of her expired passport loomed like a dark cloud, another headache she desperately tried not to focus on.

The small, bright orange hotel lobby, usually filled with bustling energy, was quiet and strangely tranquil for a change. A sense of relief washed over her for just a fleeting moment; normally, the air would be heavy with the sounds of staff engaging in loud conversations, children crying, and a variety of unseemly noises echoing from more than one room. But today, it felt unnervingly calm, the silence only heightening her distress.

"Jesas, help me," she uttered under her breath, her voice barely a whisper, hoping for a glimmer of solace in these trying times.

Rena walked with an air of grace and unyielding confidence as she approached the office, determined not to reveal the nervous wreck she felt simmering just beneath the surface. She certainly wasn't going to show them even a hint of her unease; after all, she had worked too hard to maintain her composure. At the very least, when they inevitably threw her out or delivered the bad news, her dignity would still remain intact.

By the time she reached the office door, her brain felt as if it was about to explode out of her skull from the overwhelming anxiety. She desperately needed to calm down and gather her thoughts. It's not as if she didn't already know what was about to transpire; the haunting dreams had been plaguing her ever since the third day of not making her payments. She was actually surprised they had waited this long to confront her.

The receptionist, with her sharp features and icy demeanor, was the only staff member present, reminding Rena of the hateful woman she had encountered at The Catalina Hotel. It felt as though she had been anticipating Rena's arrival, as she pointed her finger toward the office door with an unmistakably malicious look before turning her back to feign an interest in her work. Rena took a deep breath and knocked on the door with a trembling hand, her heart racing in her chest.

"Come in," a voice she didn't recognize responded, speaking in perfect English. She had been expecting Alphonso, the floor manager, who had always been much more understanding in tense situations. Instead, this unfamiliar voice sent her already elevated stress level soaring through the roof. As she pushed the door open and stepped into the room, a short man stood up abruptly, extending a hand to greet her.

"Hi, I am Miguel. It's a pleasure to meet you." He held out his hand, and she took it hesitantly. A feeling of relief washed over her like a gentle wave.

"I'm Rena, nice to meet you as well."

"Have a seat, Rena," he instructed kindly, his tone unmistakably American.

"Thank you," Rena breathed out, feeling a surge of gratitude that he wasn't going to attack her while she was standing there on shaky legs. The thought of that made her uneasy, and she didn't think she could have stood it for much longer.

"What's going on? Is everything okay with you?"

She understood exactly what he was asking. It was the same concern that Alphonso had voiced to her several months ago, and it lingered in her mind.

"I'm really sorry that I am taking so long to pay you, but I can't seem to find any of my friends who were helping me overcome this situation. I am also trying to find a job online, but it seems to be an incredibly difficult task."

Rena took her phone out and shoved it towards him, displaying her Amazon account to show him the books she had written and posted on the platform. "I write books and sell them on Amazon, but honestly, they're not doing so well at the moment."

He took her phone and glanced through the various books that proudly displayed her name on their covers. For a brief moment, he appeared genuinely impressed by her accomplishments.

"My associates want me to send you away, but I'm fully aware of what many people are struggling with right now. It's incredibly difficult for everyone all around," he paused thoughtfully, passing her phone back to her with a measured grace. "I'm going to give you a few more days. If in that time you haven't managed to come up with the necessary funds, I will regrettably have to go along with what my associates suggest."

Rena felt an overwhelming sense of relief wash over her. The threat of being thrown out was averted —at least for now.

"Thank you so much. I believe I should be able to secure the funds by then. Thank you," she said earnestly.

He looked at her, nodding his head slightly, a gesture that seemed to signal her dismissal.

As she left his office, she felt surprisingly light on her feet. The headache was still pounding relentlessly, but her heartbeat was gradually returning to a calmer rhythm.

Back in her room, she cradled her head in her hands and silently thanked Source for coming through for her in this trying moment. She picked up her phone and began calling and texting all those who had been supportive since the pandemic had initially started, but to her dismay, there was no response. Deciding to take it one day at a time, she sat down on the edge of her bed and made a conscious effort to calm herself. The headache was slowly subsiding, yet her stress level remained distressingly elevated.

It was early evening, a tranquil moment in the day. The last remnants of food had been consumed yesterday, but she still had a small supply of water and a bit of coffee remaining. With a sense of routine, she prepared herself a comforting cup of coffee and moved to straighten her makeshift bed in the bathroom. The hotel remained enveloped in a calm and quiet atmosphere, a stark contrast to the chaos she had experienced earlier.

Going to bed early sounded incredibly appealing to her, offering a respite from the overwhelming stimulation of negative energy that had left her feeling achingly light and weary. Choosing to disregard everything around her, Rena gently rocked herself into a fitful sleep. It was after one in the early morning when she finally woke up, feeling disoriented. It was too early to rise and tackle any tasks, yet too late to reach out with calls or texts to anyone whom she might normally contact. To pass the time, she turned to YouTube, losing herself in the mindless scrolling. Before she knew it, the cheerful chattering of birds began to pierce her slumber, bringing her back to awareness. Rena attempted to stave off the paralyzing fear of the unknown looming before her, but the suffocating dread was insurmountable.

The excruciating fear that began creeping into her soul started building around three in the morning. She tried to send desperate mental messages to Luke, fully aware of exactly where he was at that very moment. With every ounce of her mental focus, she pleaded silently for his help, but it seemed he was resolutely ignoring her. He had truly meant it when he said she should go and find another man, which only fueled her anger. Leaving her body to travel to him took only a matter of seconds, and she arrived just in time to witness him checking his messages and callously deleting hers without a second thought.

Luke sold drugs of all sorts, from the most harmless substances to those that held a darker reputation. Giving her a mere ten dollars a day to cover her hotel expenses would be like throwing pennies into a bottomless pit, insignificant compared to the countless hundred dollar bills he was stacking up. She was so furious with him that, in a fit of righteous indignation, she appeared right there in front of him, sitting crosslegged on his messy center table.

He suddenly jolted upright, staring at her with his mouth agape and eyes wide with genuine shock. She felt an overwhelming urge to take something heavy and strike him across the head with it, but, frustratingly, she couldn't bring herself to do so. Instead, she simply faded away. Back in her hotel room, she texted him again, her frustration mounting when nothing came back. She desperately tried to send mental messages to her other friends, but still, nobody responded. Everyone seemed to be going through their own struggles. Financial issues were rampant; money was tight, and nobody appeared to be in a position to spend or show any charitable inclination, she summarized with a heavy heart.

It had been three long days since she last communicated with Miguel, and the hotel, once a haven of peace, had returned to its noisy state. This cacophony, she learned, was a direct result of his absence, and it only deepened her sense of hopelessness. Rena decided she needed to reach out and ask her tree friends for assistance. It was still early in the morning, and the birds flitted around excitedly, anticipating the warmth of the sunrise.

"*I don't have any money for food,*" she confessed to them, her voice tinged with desperation. "*Will you help me?*"

They were still shrouded in residual darkness, and she couldn't visually perceive them. However, she sensed their presence, felt their energy mingling with the vibrant excitement radiating from the birds outside. Yet, nobody said anything in response to her plea. They probably had never had a human ask them for help before, and the silence hung heavily in the air. Rena let out a deep sigh and returned to the bathroom, feeling the weight of her hunger pressing down on her like a lead blanket. She was teetering on the threshold of what she could endure without food. She had never gone longer than three days without a meal, and only during her time in Mexico had she ever experienced such hunger.

Her water supply had completely run out, and with no food available, she made the desperate decision to see if she could go at least a week without nourishment. After all, what was a week compared to the greater struggles others had endured? Jesus had famously gone forty days and forty nights without a single bite to eat. Yet, by the fifth day, she was faced with the painful reality that passing her stool had become excruciatingly difficult, prompting her to stop trying altogether. She had also ceased showering, as she questioned the very point of such an exercise in her current state.

By the tenth day, she had essentially surrendered herself to the inevitability of death by starvation, with neither food nor water to sustain her. As she lay there, she counted her blessings whenever she didn't hear anything from Miguel, fervently praying that her friends were somehow managing to stay safe and well.

In one haunting dream, she had imagined that her dear friend Kimmy had caught Covid-19 and tragically passed away, a revelation that struck her heart with such strength that it nearly crippled her when she awoke the following morning, she found her pillow drenched in tears from her night of torment.

"Hi. Hi," she suddenly heard Matilda greet loudly several times, but she had sunk too deeply into her sorrow to muster the energy to respond or even get up to acknowledge her. Furthermore, she was far too exhausted and weak to even consider intervening in whatever situation was unfolding outside.

Just fifteen minutes later, the agonizing cries of two children pierced through her fog of despair, one child's voice screaming louder than the other. She knew she would hate herself later for not mustering the strength to try harder, but in her current condition, she could hardly fathom what she could possibly do.

By the fourteenth day of her ordeal, she had lost an alarming amount of weight, to the point where she could barely stand upright. It made her wonder how in the world Jesus had managed to endure forty days and forty nights in the unforgiving wilderness without food or water. Fourteen days in, and she was already on the verge of expiring.

Her exhausted brain felt like it was about to shut down completely as she registered the unnerving quiet and eerie calmness of the hotel surrounding her. Her weakened heart began to race, pounding rapidly in her chest, while her body shook uncontrollably with fear and a sense of helpless anticipation. She was about to be dragged out of the hotel, far from her current situation, while she was too weak to even lift her own luggage.

Why had the water chased her all the way to Mexico? And why had she ever thought Mexico was a good place to escape to and try to build a new life? In any other circumstance, her overwhelming regret would have consumed her, but in her current condition, it was merely a dull ache in the back of her mind.

When the knock finally came, it took every ounce of strength she had left to muster the courage to stand up. Slowly and unsteadily, she made her way to the door, each step feeling like a monumental effort. Rosa was standing there, her eyes wide with shock. She took one quick look at Rena, filled with disbelief, and then ran down the hallway to the office.

Rena couldn't imagine what the hotel helper must have seen that caused such a reaction. This was the very first time in her life that she had ever gone this long without food, and the isolation weighed heavily on her. With no one to help and the limited number of friends she had drifting away, she felt utterly abandoned and fearful of what was to come next. Shakily, she turned and walked back to the bathroom, intentionally avoiding any glance in the direction of her tree friend. In fact, she had kept the curtains tightly closed, unwilling to face the reality of her surroundings. She craved to suffer in silence, away from the world that had become so indifferent to her plight.

Two hours later, a persistent knock resounded on her door once again. Wishing more than anything that they would simply leave her to fade away in peace, she begrudgingly got up—feeling as if she were an elderly woman of eighty, with every part of her body seemingly buried deep in the grave—and slowly made her way to the door. To her surprise, it was Rosa standing there, holding a colorful basket filled with fresh fruits, vibrant vegetables, and a large bottle of refreshing water.

Rena, feeling far too weak to even attempt to hold the heavy basket, watched as Rosa kindly stepped inside and set it down for her.

"Muchísimo gracias," Rena managed to utter, her voice barely above a whisper, as she could hardly make the words come out in her current state.

"You're welcome," Rosa replied, her tone warm but hurried, as she tried to escape the room as fast as she could, eager to let Rena have her moment.

Rena had been avoiding the mirror for quite some time; however, seeing Rosa's shocked reaction to her appearance again, motivated her to confront the truth. She approached the mirror and was met with a horrifying sight—she could hardly believe that the gaunt figure staring back at her was indeed herself. The thing in the mirror was nothing but skin and bones. Fourteen days of this torment had transformed her, and she pondered somberly what Jesus must have looked like after forty days in the wilderness. She simply couldn't begin to imagine.

The Jamaican

"THE TREES MAY NOT HAVE EYES LIKE US, BUT THEY'RE SEEING EVERYTHING, EVEN THE DUST."

"THE TREES MAY NOT HAVE EARS LIKE US, BUT THEY'RE LISTENING TO EVERYTHING, EVEN WHEN WE FIGHT AND CUSS."

"THE TREES MAY NOT HAVE MOUTH LIKE US, BUT THEY EAT, SPEAK AND NEVER MAKE FUSS."

"THE TREES MAY NOT HAVE FEET LIKE US, BUT THEY'RE WALKING, EVEN WHILE YOU CATCH THE BUS."

Chapter 14
THE FRYING PAN

The very first thing she brought to her mouth was a plump, ripe tomato. She couldn't quite explain it, but perhaps it was because the six big, red tomatoes sitting enticingly in the basket looked incredibly delicious to her at that moment. She was well aware of their high nutritional value and figured that consuming one would revive her the fastest and boost her energy. Tentatively, she took a bite, but instantly felt a wave of nausea wash over her, making her feel like she might throw up. In a panic, she dashed to the toilet and waited, hoping for relief. But nothing came. Crawling back to her makeshift bed felt like a small victory, bringing her a sense of comfort as she lay down. Her body had never felt this way before—like a whisper from death itself.

Every nerve ending was trembling with unease, and she was overwhelmed by a profound lack of focus. Her body, once her own, now felt foreign and unresponsive. Eventually, sleep overtook her weary mind. Two hours later, she stirred awake and took another bite of the tomato, but unlike before, nausea didn't overwhelm her this time. Yet, she still felt suspended at death's door, teetering on the edge of consciousness.

    Faint voices were drifting in from somewhere nearby. To her disorientation, it sounded as though they were right in the bathroom with her, but she was far too sleepy to muster the strength to see who they were. Suddenly, someone flipped her over, roughly. Startled, she opened her eyes wide. To her utter shock, there were five men surrounding her, invading her personal space. One of them was hastily busy undressing her before he quickly pulled down his pants with an unsettling urgency. She screamed, but no sound came out. Rena began to fight back instinctively, but she couldn't feel her body—every muscle was heavy and unresponsive. With horror, she watched as the man climbed on top of her and forcibly inserted his penis into her. After he was finished, another man stepped forward to do the same. One after another, they violated her, taking their pleasure without regard. All the while, she kept repeating to herself, "it's only a dream," trying to convince herself of her own fabrication of reality. Then, another man entered the bathroom, adding to the chaos.

"Please God, let them stop," she pleaded desperately.

"That's enough! Get out!" The last male commanded, his voice laced with anger. Rena watched, her heart pounding, as they vanished through the window, their presence lingering like a nightmare. The furious male lingered for a brief moment, looking down at her with a flicker of regret etched on his features before he finally exited the room.

As Rena woke up at twilight, the haunting scene replayed in her mind, compelling her to survey her surroundings in search of any evidence left by the intruders. To her relief, nothing seemed out of the ordinary. She noticed she was still wearing the same clothes she hadn't bothered to change for nearly two weeks, a testament to her emotional and physical turmoil. The scent and the memory of the five males who had violated her remained vividly imprinted in her thoughts, making it difficult to dismiss them as nothing more than a horrific dream. Gathering her strength, she willed herself to rise.

Though her body felt severely weakened, she recognized the urgent need for a bath and a fresh change of clothing. However, washing herself proved to be a slow and arduous task given her fragile state. Once she finally completed her bath and dressed in clean clothes, Rena turned her attention to changing the sheets. As she began the task, a wave of dizziness washed over her, compelling her to pause and steady herself for a moment before continuing with her chores.

Going to the stove, she carefully plugged it in and set a small amount of water in the smallest of the blue pots. After rummaging through the basket, she decided to add a quarter of the fresh lettuce she found, along with some onions that she diligently diced. Tipping a pinch of salt into the pot, followed by a sprinkle of black pepper, she allowed it to boil for a minute before taking a tentative sip of the simmering broth. She could only manage to swallow a few mouthfuls before the nauseating feeling returned with a vengeance, overwhelming her senses. Instead of making her way to the bathroom, she chose to sit down on the edge of the bed and held her head down in an attempt to collect her thoughts and settle her stomach. After ten long minutes in that position, she felt a slight alleviation of discomfort, prompting her to drift back to sleep on the makeshift bed in the bathroom.

Her body in state of refusal, didn't seem to want anything else, though it was still shaking slightly from weakness. On the third day of drinking lettuce broth, she was finally able to pee again; the relief was dampened, though, as it came out just as painfully as before.

By the fifth day, she was starting to feel a lot better.

A sudden knock disturbed the silence of her room. It was Rosa, standing there with purpose, reading off her phone, "You need to go to the office."

Rena nodded her head obediently. She was clean and somewhat put together, despite the sunken dark circles that lingered around her exhausted eyes and the loose, swinging pants and t-shirt she wore. She slowly walked toward the office, no longer radiating confidence, with her back bent and head bowed somberly. The nausea she had fought so valiantly against now attacked her full on, as cold sweat and tremors racked her frail frame.

"I'm a strong woman. I'm a strong woman. I'm a strong woman," she repeated in her mind, clinging to her mantra as she desperately tried to fend off the sickness and the fear that threatened to corner her like a predator.

Miguel took one quick glance at her and tried his hardest not to show his shock at her fragile state.

"I'm sorry I couldn't find anyone," she murmured softly, pity lacing her voice.

"It's okay, don't worry. You can stay here as long as you like. Don't worry." His accent was now a strong Mexican accent, a beautiful reminder of his heritage. All pretense of Americanism left him completely at the sight of Rena's frail, skeletal frame that was distressingly visible beneath her pale dark skin.

She was trying very hard to stifle any visible signs of her tears, as the feeling of self-pity overwhelmed her completely.

"If you run out of food at any time, just come here and get whatever you need. Whatever you want, just tell them and they will get it for you."

Rena opened her mouth to say something, to express her gratitude, but he continued speaking, gently.

"Don't worry. I understand that many people are going through a lot. Don't worry."

"Thank you," she told him, fighting back the urge to fall apart at his kindness and generosity.

It took another full week for her weary body and troubled mind to return to some semblance of homeostasis. Although she never fully regained all the weight she had lost, she was no longer looking like a mere skeleton, which filled her with relief. Rena was immensely grateful to Miguel for his generous and compassionate heart. As she gradually gathered her strength each day, she would leave her body in a focused attempt to teach her spirit how to lift objects around her. She started with lighter items, painstakingly progressing to heavier ones as her confidence grew. With constant training and a committed determination, making sure not to leave her vessel for any long duration, she was eventually able to master lifting the heavy ottoman that rested in the corner of the room.

It was a full month after she finally regained her much-needed strength that she had firmly decided to pay Luke another surprise visit. A Saturday, precisely at midnight, Eastern Standard Time, to be exact. This was the time she knew with certainty that he would be relaxing in his living room, sprawled out on the incredibly ugly sofa she had persistently tried to convince him to avoid purchasing. As she tiptoed in, she found him fast asleep. His hefty body sank deep into the sagging cushions of the old sofa, while his overgrown belly hung perilously over the side in a rather comical fashion.

She walked quietly past him into the kitchen, searching for the heaviest frying pan she could find. After a moment of rummaging, she finally located one, then went to hover over him, making sure to position herself in such a way that it appeared as if the frying pan was magically suspended in midair. With a playful yet gentle tap on his forehead, she aimed to rouse him from his slumber, before energetically flipping on the light switch to illuminate the space around them.

He blinked in confusion, gazing at the frying pan seemingly floating towards him, and instinctively turned to bury his face in the back of the sofa. Rena knew he believed he was merely caught in a vivid dream, so with determination, she took advantage of the moment and whacked him across the back of his head with the frying pan. He sat up in shock, rubbing the sore spot on his head, before he jumped up and fled in fright up the stairs, nearly tripping over himself as he went.

The frying pan, in a comedic yet relentless manner, pursued him all the way to the top of the stairs and delivered another swift smack to the back of his head. He burst into the room, desperately attempting to slam the door closed behind him, but he wasn't quick enough; the frying pan made a dramatic entrance right along with him. It smacked him sharply across his jaw, causing him to fall to his knees, his hands clasped together in a pleading gesture.

"Jesus, I'm really sorry! I'll stopped selling drugs to people. Please forgive me; I know what I've been doing is wrong. Please, I'm begging you, forgive me. Forgive me. Lord Jesus, please, forgive me!"

He was in a complete, full bowed position, his body trembling slightly, but Lena had no mercy for him whatsoever. She had nearly perished from the agony of starvation because he had been too stingy to extend a helping hand. With a surge of frustration, she delivered another hard whack to the back of his head, the sound ringing in the otherwise quiet room.

"Oh Lord, I promise, you boy won't dare to do it again!" He exclaimed emphatically. As he instinctively put his hands over his head to shield himself from the relentless assault of the frying pan, he began to pray earnestly, seeking divine intervention.

Rena threw down the frying pan beside his overstuffed, bowing frame with a resounding clang against the wooden floor, the noise echoing in the stark stillness.

He remained in the bowed position for an agonizing two more minutes, mumbling soft, desperate pleas to Jesus.

"You can get up now," she finally instructed, her voice steady. She was perched on the only chair in the cramped bedroom, looking as if she owned the place.

Luke stood up awkwardly, his movements clumsy and hesitant. He looked at her wide-eyed, as if he was about to have a heart attack from the vision that confront him.

"The next time I come here, you will not live to tell the tale," she warned him in a calm, almost bemused tone, before she vanished from sight like a wisp of smoke.

Once back in her room, Lena felt a surge of triumph filling her spirit. She couldn't quite believe she had just done that to him. With a spark of glee, she picked up her phone and texted him, her heart racing with anticipation. A couple of seconds later, his reply came through, and to her astonishment, he sent her a thousand dollars without hesitation.

"That harse!" She whispered to herself, realizing she should have learned this trick a long time ago.

Rena travelled to the Pedophilia Hacker's room situated directly above her own, arriving just in time to witness the last remnants of the message from her phone fading away from his computer screen. The small space was devoid of any trace of his personhood, starkly empty and eerily silent. With a sense of urgent determination, she approached the desk and filled the large cup he had left there with water, then poured it over the computer in a wild, reckless motion. The machine didn't short-circuit quickly enough to meet her expectations. Frustrated yet fueled by adrenaline, she seized the chair and forcefully smashed it against the computers and the desk, heedless of the destruction she was causing. Satisfied that everything was irreparably wrecked, she astral travelled back to her own room.

A wave of happiness washed over her as she descended the stairs to clear up her financial affairs, cheerfully paying off all her past bills and for the month ahead.

To her delight, another five hundred dollars appeared in her account, prompting her to laugh aloud at the unexpected amount. She really had given him a substantial scare. He certainly deserved every bit of it. Yet, before she could linger on that thought, an unsettling image invaded her mind, and in a daze, she found herself back in her old apartment on Kensington Avenue in Buffalo. There lay that loathsome cocksucker, tightly wrapped around his male lover, the infamous old pimp—both of them sprawled carelessly across her bed, deep in sleep.

Determined to act, she navigated to the kitchen to retrieve the meat chopper, its steel glinting ominously in the dim light. Returning with the heavy utensil, she loomed over Behanzin's bare and unsuspecting body, her heart racing as she allowed herself a few more lingering moments of contemplation before bringing the chopper crashing down, splitting his head open in a gruesome display of power. The muffled noise that attempted to escape his lips was swiftly silenced. Not pausing for breath, she whirled to face the old lover next, brutally severing his oversized cock and forcefully stuffing it into his mouth, silencing his panicked screams into a guttural growl.

Before he could comprehend what was happening, she slashed deeply into his chest, slicing him open all the way down to his belly button and leaving his insides grotesquely exposed. Taking a deliberate step backward, one hand confidently resting on her hip while the other tightly gripped the meat chopper, she watched intently as blood and intestines spilled like a crimson waterfall onto the once-pristine bedspread.

The chaotic and bloody tableau she had created was doing something transformative to the dark monster her being was evolving into—or perhaps it had always been there, lying dormant. She didn't care to ponder the moral implications, instead reveling in the exhilarating thrill of her actions; her being was experiencing a level of excitement and liberation it had not felt in what seemed like an eternity.

She nodded her head slowly at the extensive destruction that surrounded her, then made her way to the kitchen to wash her hands thoroughly, the warm water a soothing balm to her triumph-filled heart. Moments later, she found herself back in her hotel room where she reveled in the intoxicating sense of victory that coursed through her veins. She had embraced the identity of the murderous bitch she had become. The thought abruptly halted her movement, freezing her in place. Yes, she was indeed a murderous bitch—an unsettling yet empowering realization. Rena continued on to the bathroom, where she took a seat on her neatly made bed, pondering her reflection and the drastic changes within her. But there truly was nothing substantial left to contemplate. Certain individuals needed to be vanquished; they had relentlessly preyed on her vulnerabilities. She was certain she wasn't the first nor was she the last to fall victim to their shameless schemes. However, for the unfortunate souls who would follow in her wake, those two would never again have the chance to torment anyone else.

It was now late in the night. Though hunger gnawed at her insides, a deep sense of satisfaction with her newfound life overshadowed it. Too energized to find sleep's embrace, Rena busied herself with researching the Jamaican Consulate and its precise location. The first order of business would be to secure herself a new passport; then she planned to indulge in a delightful meal at a fancy restaurant, something she hadn't been able to enjoy since her arrival in beautiful Mexico.

While she was engrossed in planning for the exciting day ahead, a bright, beaming light suddenly burst into the room, capturing her attention. She watched it with unwavering curiosity, unafraid. After all she had just accomplished, she would never again let fear control her life—or anyone or anything. Spiraling in the intoxicating thrill of her murderous transformation, she observed as the brilliant light gradually faded away, revealing the striking female entity who had visited her some time prior.

Ananuyah.

Rena's face broke into a huge smile, a radiant expression of welcome, as she embraced the presence of the woman who had returned.

Ananuyah slowly stretched out her hand, her fingers trembling slightly with anticipation, and Rena instinctively took it. In an instant, they both disappeared from the claustrophobic confines of the cramped space, leaving behind her body, which sagged and became lifeless on the makeshift bed, a silent testament to their abrupt departure.

Chapter 15
MEETING LENA

Rena found herself stepping into the expansive halls of the Metropolitan Museum, a place that never failed to ignite her sense of wonder. She had only visited this illustrious museum twice before, once with a large group from her college, where the experience, though pleasant, felt somewhat constrained by the collective schedule. This time, however, she was free to explore at her own pace, reveling in the possibility of unearthing hidden knowledge.

As she looked around, noticing she was surrounded by patrons of the arts, a vibrant tapestry of individuals representing various ethnicities, sizes, and distinct dress codes. The soft whispering voices and delicate strains of Bach's classical music playing in the background combined beautifully to create a quiet yet excited ambiance that enveloped her. Rena moved gracefully from gallery to gallery, admiring the meticulously curated displays and the noteworthy artworks alongside elegantly dressed visitors. Their laughter and nonchalant attitude began to elevate her own mood, and for just a fleeting moment, she felt herself becoming more whole and content.

Eventually, she walked into the grand room where Michelangelo's breathtaking sculptures were on display, alongside other renowned masterpieces from the same illustrious period. Despite the beauty all around her, the space was quite crowded, much to her dismay. She attempted to muster excitement for this particular area, even though she wasn't particularly fond of large crowds. The last two times she had been there, it had not been nearly as packed, allowing for a more intimate experience with the art and the atmosphere.

Trying not to bump into anyone, she looked around and noticed for the first time that no one was wearing a mask. How was it possible? With everything under lock down due to COVID-19, she was here among a large group of people who seemed unconcerned about the virus. The rich and famous from all over the world did not seem concerned that they might catch something and die. She was freaking out. How could she not have noticed?

She looked around for Ananuyah, but after several moments, she realized there was no sign of her anywhere, leading to a slight sense of disappointment. Rena shrugged her shoulders in acceptance, recognizing that sometimes things simply don't go as planned. If she was going to die of COVID-19, especially having just recovered from a grueling fourteen-day period of starvation, then so it shall be. After all, she was present in this moment, so she might as well enjoy whatever life had to offer her right now.

Rena took a deep breath to calm herself, adopting a "when in Rome, do what the Romans do" mentality as she tried to embrace the atmosphere around her.

"You look so beautiful," Ananuyah said from somewhere behind her. Rena turned around, expecting to see someone else the woman might be talking to, but instead, she was met with the astonishing sight of Ananuyah, who was elegantly dressed in a very expensively designed green satin evening gown, adorned with real diamonds that beautifully decorated the sleeveless bodice. Teardrop diamond earrings hung gracefully from her ears, and her dazzling face had been skillfully made up to perfection. Her jet black hair, which was parted perfectly halfway down the middle, shone brilliantly, flowing straight down to her waist. In that moment, Rena couldn't help but think she was more stunning than a Nubian Barbie doll.

"Wow! You look absolutely amazing." All her worries about catching COVID-19 vanished completely from her mind as she took in the stunning sight of the diamond-studded stilettos and the perfectly coordinated clutch purse, which beautifully complemented Ananuyah's glamorous ensemble.

"You look stunning yourself," came the reply, filled with genuine warmth and heartfelt appreciation.

"What!" Rena exclaimed, her eyes widening as she looked down at her bare feet, which she tended to use for her astral travels, only to notice they were now elegantly clad in dainty red stilettos adorned with dazzling diamond studs all over. She was pleasantly surprised to find her toenails painted beautifully, each foot adorned with a delicately crafted diamond ring on her middle toe. Her floor-length, off-the-shoulder, red satin dress showcased a daring side split that went all the way up to the top of her thigh, exuding both sophistication and allure. As she noticed the exquisite bracelet on her wrist, Rena instinctively held out her hand to admire the fragile-looking diamonds elegantly housed in rose gold, perfectly matching her stunning dress. She silently prayed that it wouldn't slip off her hand and disappear. She couldn't see herself as clearly as her friend was seeing her, so she struggled to grasp the true loveliness she represented in that moment.

"Why did we come here?" she asked, her curiosity piqued.

"It's to reward you for what you did," Ananuyah replied cryptically.

"What did I do?" Rena inquired, trying hard to think back. Except for becoming a murderess, she couldn't seem to recall anything else of significance.

"No human has ever been able to teach themselves what you have so remarkably taught yourself and succeeded. Your mom was the only one in over two thousand years to achieve such feats. And yet, she did not progress at the impressive rate you did."

"Oh! I didn't know it took special talents."

Rena shrugged her shoulders lightly, feeling a mix of curiosity and amusement, before she turned to take a refreshing glass of red wine from a passing waiter gliding through the crowd. She took a generous sip, discovering that it was her all-time favorite Jamaican Red Label Wine—the original, full-bodied taste that always delighted her senses.

They were making their way towards the large, elaborately decorated dining area, which boasted an enticing buffet spread filled with an array of colorful dishes.

"It's a very difficult feat for living humans, but here you are, holding your wine and seamlessly blending in," Ananuyah remarked, her eyes sparkling with intrigue.

Rena didn't quite understand what the big fuss was all about, feeling a hint of skepticism creeping in. "Aren't these people afraid of catching COVID-19?" she asked, changing the subject in an attempt to divert her thoughts.

"You haven't figured it out yet?" Ananuyah replied with a knowing grin.

Before Rena could respond, an overwhelming feeling of being pulled towards the exit washed over her, compelling her to act. She let herself go, surrendering to the sensation.

Rena had learned early on in her experience that whenever the inexplicable pull came on, she should simply let go and follow it. She relaxed her mind, allowing her being to be drawn into a dark room within the museum. It was devoid of people, yet rich with carvings of sleeping angels that seemed to whisper secrets of a forgotten time. The intricate carvings looked incredibly lifelike, and Rena found it strange that no one else was present to admire these exquisite statues.

Each angel was captured in various poses, much like the visitors in the other spaces, their diverse ethnicities, sizes, and colors reflecting a beautiful spectrum of humanity. She slowly walked from one statue to another, absorbing the details and reading the inscriptions with admiration. Yet, something within her stirred with impatience; she felt herself being irresistibly dragged across the room to the largest of the statues, the most captivating and lifelike of them all. It lay there as if sleeping, peaceful and serene.

Rena stood transfixed, watching it intently, almost expecting it to open its eyes and blink at her, bridging the gap between the living and the ethereal.

A sudden, jarring cracking noise drew her attention to the floor where the statue lay peacefully, oblivious to the chaos surrounding it. To her astonishment, the intricately detailed carving began to break open, and a woman emerged, crawling out slowly. The woman had short, salt and pepper afro kinky hair plastered to her scalp, weighed down by a jellylike substance that covered her entire body. Her clothing, seemingly from another world, was stuck tightly to her, while her very dark skin dripped with the sticky, gooey substance.

"Chile, help mi get dem things off me," the woman implored with urgency. Her unnaturally snow white eyes, sharply contrasted by her yellow irises, bore into Rena, as if searching her very soul.

The sight of them shocked Rena into a blank stare, causing her to feel as though she were going into a convulsion, her eyes rolling over and her head becoming so weightless that she could hardly process what was happening.

"Hold mi hand dem pickiney. Hurry up, mi nuh have all day to waste," the woman insisted, her tone far from gentle, filled with an unsettling impatience. But Rena felt as if she were being swallowed up by the strange atmosphere; she simply couldn't do what the woman was demanding.

The woman, seemingly determined, reached out her hand and grasped for Rena's, her fingers slick with the gelatinous substance.

"Snap out of it, chile," she urged, her voice breaking through Rena's fog of confusion.

Rena felt the cold, sticky hand touching hers, and a wave of clarity washed over her momentarily, pulling her back to her senses. She glanced around the dimly lit room to see if all the other angel statues had also sent forth salt and pepper-haired middle-aged women into the world. To her dismay, the room was completely empty, void of all the previous carvings—including the cocoon-like structure from which the woman had emerged. The large, dark, and now empty room suddenly felt vibrantly alive, filling Rena's heart with an inexplicable fear that quickened her pulse and sent shivers down her spine.

Where was Ananuyah? If only she could see the ominous beam of light. Her breathing was coming out shallow and quick while the desperate need to escape the confines of the room grew stronger by the second.

She had completely forgotten that she was a non-material, murderous force of nature who feared nothing; yet, she still felt tethered to her human form. This tenuous connection was wreaking havoc on her spirit, leaving her disoriented and frantic. Suddenly, everything became too much, and she fainted.

Rena woke up to find herself back in her physical vessel, lying on the plush hotel bed, the soft sheets cradling her. The clock on the bedside table showed it was just before five in the morning. She got up slowly, making her way to the kitchen to drink a glass of water, trying desperately not to dwell on the disconcerting experience she had just endured.

What had happened to the enigmatic salt-and-pepper-haired woman? She wondered as she trudged to the bathroom, determined to make her bed and catch a little nap before preparing for her anticipated rendezvous.

"I'm right here," the woman said, suddenly appearing out of thin air.

She was now gently stroking Matilda, the cat who was wrapped comfortably in her arms. Rena looked closely at the dark-skinned woman whose hair was no longer short and grey but had transformed to the brilliant color of freshly fallen snow. The length of her hair cascaded past her knees, flowing like a silken waterfall. Her skin had smoothed out, and she no longer appeared to be in middle age but rather closer to the youthful look of someone near thirty. The only element that remained the same were her striking eyes. Well, that's not entirely accurate; the entire left eye was the color of her hair with a mesmerizing yellow iris, while the right eye mirrored the color of the sky on a cloudless day, decorated with a peculiar purple iris. She was a strange and captivating beauty that Rena couldn't seem to tear her gaze away from.

"Who are you? And why did you come out of that statue?" Rena asked, her voice tinged with confusion.

"I'm surprised you haven't recognized me yet, sister," the woman said, still gently stroking the traitorous cat, her demeanor both unsettling and alluring.

"Sister?"

"Yes! I'm Lena. We lived together for a brief

moment, but when you transitioned to this dimension, Mumma and I ended up in another dimension entirely."

Rena looked intently at the being sitting gracefully in her room, as if she had been there all along, quietly observing her.

"Another dimension?"

"Yes! Another dimension," Lena exclaimed, her face lighting up with a smile so radiant that it caused Rena to feel a lump of conflicting emotions swell in her chest. With careful grace and mindfulness, Lena got up without disturbing the sleeping cat curled up peacefully on her lap. Gliding to the window like a whisper on the breeze, she effortlessly removed the clothes pin without even using her hands, then opened the curtains wide.

It was not yet sunny outside, casting a muted light through the panes. Rena could hardly make out her friends in the distance, but she could sense something was distinctly off about the scene; they appeared to be trembling, even though the stillness of the air indicated there was no breeze.

The surrounding trees stood rigid, and the birds flitted around erratically, their chaotic movements a stark contrast to the eerie calmness of the other trees. It was far too early in the in the morning for them to be in such a frenzied state, and Rena had never seen them like this before. Turning to the being—who claimed with confidence to be her sister—she regarded her with increasing suspicion.

"They are my friends; please leave them alone."

"I'm not doing anything," Lena replied, her voice too innocent, as she deftly flipped her pointy finger against her thumb, causing all her tree friends to vanish into thin air.

Rena instinctively recalled her twin sister, who tragically died at birth. She saw vividly in her mind every single incident that had taken place within the confines of their mother's womb. She remembered the playful fighting, the joyful laughter, the innocent playing, and the soothing tones of their mother's voice echoing around them, wrapping them in a warm embrace. The memories flooded her, bringing forth the dreams that had haunted her nights, dreams filled with fleeting visions and visitations from her sister. She watched in captivated wonder as her sister flicked her fingers gracefully, returning her gathered friends back to their rightful places in the natural world.

The birds, however, seemed indifferent to those calls, refusing to return to their nests, with the exception of a lone, strikingly bright yellow butterfly that glided by. Its large presence felt oddly misplaced in the cool air of the early morning.

"*I'm really sorry*," Rena sent quietly to the swaying trees, before turning her back on them to fully face her sister.

"So why are you here now? What is it that you truly want from me?"

Lena's expression was filled with rage, making Rena's heart race.

"Mumma is missing! And you are the last one to see her," she accused, her eyes blazing.

"What the hell! I don't know what you're talking about," Rena exclaimed, confusion lacing her voice.

"You remember crying and pleading to SOURCE to help the boy. You saw her. You were in the room with her!" Lena shot back, her voice intense with urgency and anger.

Rena struggled to recall that moment, but then, a vivid image appeared—she remembered the flickering being who had held the boy snugly under her arm. The likeness she had thought belonged to Sarai suddenly came into sharper focus.

"That was Mumma?" Rena gasped, disbelief washing over her. Her mother, the woman she had only met once, when she first entered the womb, was right there in front of her, and she hadn't even recognized her. "Oh my God! That was my mother?" she uttered in shock, unable to process the revelation.

Lena had put a thin, yet effective, membrane of acoustic material carefully wrapped around them to prevent any sound from escaping into the outside world. She was all too aware of her sister's loudness, which could easily attract unwanted attention.

Rena found herself recalling the woman who had winked at her, yet she still could not wrap her mind around the fact that woman was actually her mother. How could she possibly not have recognized her own mother? The woman had such enchanting, laughing eyes, brimming with mischief and warmth.

"Fuck it!!" she shouted, her voice echoing through the silence. "Fuck it, fuck it, fuck it!" Rena looked at her ethereal sister and pondered the question of where a transient being like her mother might have disappeared to. The flickering apparition—her mother—radiated an aura of immense power. She certainly didn't appear to be someone who could be easily overcome or dismissed.

While she was lost in thought, her sister's attention was abruptly captured by something happening next door. Rena, unable to see through walls in her current physical form, was taken by surprise when Lena suddenly grabbed her hand and, with an almost otherworldly strength, dragged her spirit out of her body and through the solid wall into the adjacent room. There, they found a man sitting on one of the bedside tables, intently trying to listen to Rena. He had a hidden camera embedded in his iPhone, unknowingly watching her from the privacy of her own room.

It wasn't until Lena released her hand that he noticed the two figures standing directly in front of him. Shocked, he barely registered what was happening before Lena lunged forward, grabbing him by the throat and lifting him effortlessly off his feet. He swung his legs desperately in mid-air, his hands scrambling to latch onto her grip, fighting against the impending strangulation.

"Who are you?" she shouted furiously in perfect Spanish, her voice laced with both fury and determination.

But the man couldn't respond; he was furiously swinging his feet in a desperate attempt to get air into his lungs. Suddenly, five men appeared out of nowhere, clad in silver and black uniforms, ready to assist the man whom Rena recognized as one of the hotel's handymen.

As she looked closer, she realized with a cold shiver that these five beings were, in fact, the same ones who had brutally raped her while she had been teetering on the brink of death due to starvation. The horrifying memory surged back, and she couldn't believe it—the vile act of brutality was real, not just a figment of her imagination. The rage within her murderess spirit flared up uncontrollably. She could feel something menacing starting to shift within it. Her fingernails elongated as if they were sharp claws, while her teeth transformed into terrifying fangs. To her fright, her neck stretched, and her form began to morph into the monstrous entity she had always feared. She saw red as the male, who had seemingly saved her, materialized out of thin air to stand defiantly beside her. He handed her a frying pan, and she felt a flicker of her former self returning as she wondered just what she was going to do with it. It's not like her assailants were mere mortals to be frightened away. But she clung to the pan nonetheless, instinctively feeling that it might offer some measure of protection.

The sight of the five beings seemed to enrage her sister Lena as much as it did her. A bolt of fury shot out from Lena's snow-white eyes, piercing ruthlessly through the handyman's right eye. He couldn't release a scream, however, because she still had a tight grasp on his throat. The five beings, poised before Lena, seemed oblivious to Rena, who quickly positioned herself in front of them, swatting the first rapist hard with the frying pan. He fell back, taken completely by surprise.

Lena, forced to release the handyman, had to turn her focus to defending herself against the third rapist, who charged at her wielding a rather thin, menacing-looking long sword. She swung the shimmering golden sword that had suddenly materialized in her hand, its sharp edge glinting ominously as it narrowly missed cutting him in half. The second rapist rushed in with a menacing glare, but fate was not on his side. His left arm was chopped clean off in a swift, precise motion by the unyielding swing of the golden sword.

Rena couldn't quite comprehend the thick, viscous goo spraying from the being's severed arm as she desperately attempted to shield herself from the relentless advances of the first and fourth rapists. The surreal scene felt like something straight out of a movie, especially as she cast a fleeting glance at her sister and the brave male who had come to her rescue, both engaged in a fierce struggle with three of her attackers. They were valiantly trying to protect the handyman who had managed to escape to the corner of the room, where he was anxiously cradling his damaged eye.

Rena expected that she would see blood and gore gushing everywhere, creating a horrific tableau. But to her astonishment, there was nothing; the fiery sword that had pierced through the handyman's eye had burned it clean, almost cauterized.

The sentient rapist who had lost his hand was sent back to his maker with a fate worse than death, while the other two assailants were still intent on maiming Lena and the heroic male fighting at her side. The men they were battling appeared to be sliced and diced all over, oozing goo with every frantic movement. But just as Lena prepared to deliver the final blow, they vanished into thin air.

"Cowards, come back!" Lena screamed in frustration, her voice echoing through the chaos. Rena was far too preoccupied to notice if the cowardly rapists had any intention of returning when, out of nowhere, Ananuyah appeared between her, the frying pan, and the first rapist. In an instant, he disappeared, leaving behind a sense of disbelief.

Lena slowly walked over to the handyman who had acted suspiciously. She was livid, her gaze piercing his remaining eye. A second later, she raised her sword and swung it, chopping his head clean off his body. Blood spurted everywhere. Wiping her sword on his clothing, she disappeared it. Rena was still watching the handyman's head roll as Lena walked towards them. Ananuyah was standing on her right, and the protector male was standing on her left.

"He was also in the room taking pictures while the other two raped the boy," Lena explained. "He was lucky to be in the bathroom when Mumma came; she didn't see him."

"And the five beings?" Rena asked.

"They're evildoers disrupting the balance in the third-dimensional human realm. Some of the men here are under their influence."

Ananuyah, along with the sixth male, disappeared. The two sisters went back to Rena's hotel room to find Rena's body lying in a heap on the floor, where it had fallen. Returning to her vessel and getting up off the floor, she watched her sister in thought. Matilda was busy chewing on what was left of the paper napkin, oblivious to the mess she was making.

"I must get going," Lena said before disappearing into thin air.

"THE TREES MAY NOT HAVE EYES LIKE US, BUT THEY'RE SEEING EVERYTHING, EVEN THE DUST."

"THE TREES MAY NOT HAVE EARS LIKE US, BUT THEY'RE LISTENING TO EVERYTHING, EVEN WHEN WE FIGHT AND CUSS."

"THE TREES MAY NOT HAVE MOUTH LIKE US, BUT THEY EAT, SPEAK AND NEVER MAKE FUSS."

"THE TREES MAY NOT HAVE FEET LIKE US, BUT THEY'RE WALKING, EVEN WHILE YOU CATCH THE BUS."

CHAPTER 16
THE DEAD BODY

◆

Rena sat on her bed in a dazed state, overwhelmed by the feeling of surrealism that had completely overtaken her, along with a disconcerting separation of mind and body. She felt capable of accomplishing so many things all at once, which filled her with an unexpected sense of power, yet simultaneously made her feel incredibly fragile. How could she possibly feel this way and yet not be completely shattered into countless pieces? The way they fought had left her in awe; she had never witnessed anything even remotely like it in real life before. A twin sister, whom she had once played and fought with in the safety of the womb, and whom she had met in what she had always assumed were just strange dreams, had suddenly emerged from the spirit realm to engage with her in ways she could scarcely comprehend. The realization of her ability to combat beings from other dimensions was both exhilarating and terrifying. And those rapists? They definitely weren't a mere figment of her imagination. Her body started to tremble, shaking uncontrollably as the memory sank in. She had been violated by five beings, yet she had tried to shrug it off as if it were just a bad dream. Who could actually do something so horrific? And who was that mysterious man who had come to her rescue?

"*Look out the window*," Tuck urged. Rena reluctantly moved toward the window, curiosity piquing as she wondered what chaos might be unfolding outside with her friends. It was daylight, yet the sun was completely obscured by thick clouds, and the birds, sensing the ominous absence of sunlight, hadn't bothered to leave the shelter of the trees. While a few had made their way back to their rightful homes, the majority remained on high alert, aware of the danger that loomed just beyond their branches and choosing to stay where they were.

As she scanned the scene below, she noticed Tuck looking up at her with an expression that was oddly strange and unsettling. His tree-like frame and human form appeared to have merged, and she couldn't shake the feeling that the human aspect reminded her of the very being who had saved her from despair.

"*Tuck, that was really you?*" His human form slowly materialized before her as she recognized his familiar, yet startling presence.

"*I'm truly sorry I didn't come to your aid sooner,*" he added with genuine remorse.

"It's okay. You came to my rescue, and that's all that truly matters. I had no idea you could transform into a human," she remarked, curiosity mingling with surprise. There was no immediate response from him.

"When you return this evening, we are going to begin your training," Tuck finally stated with a sense of seriousness.

"Training?" she echoed, her heart racing slightly at the thought.

"Yes. You'll need to learn how to defend yourself now more than ever," he emphasized with unwavering conviction.

Rena fully understood the implication behind his words and nodded her head in agreement, determination sparkling in her eyes. She stepped away from the window, feeling grateful that the unexpected distraction had shifted her focus away from her own swirling thoughts. With newfound urgency, she began moving swiftly, knowing that so many elements of her life were becoming clearer now that she had opened up to the reality of her situation.

Training. The reality that Tuck was going to teach her how to fight filled her with both trepidation and excitement. She worked to clear her mind as she prepared for her upcoming trip to the embassy and thought about the lunch that awaited her afterward.

She was also planning on making a quick stop at the supermarket later that day. The chips, instant noodles, and other unhealthy junk food she had been subsisting on for quite some time only managed to temporarily stall her gnawing hunger, but they were undoubtedly bad for her body and well-being.

Although she felt a deep sense of gratitude toward Miguel for his kindness, she couldn't help but desperately miss some good old-fashioned, wholesome, healthy food that would nourish her.

The sudden sound of running feet and excited voices echoing in the hallway caught her attention and momentarily startled her.

"Oh shit!" She realized with a jolt that she had completely forgotten about the dead body with the severed head in the adjoining room. For a fleeting moment, she considered throwing herself onto the bed and pretending to be asleep, given that it was still quite early in the morning. However, the reality was that she needed to prepare herself for the embassy appointment ahead.

Choosing practicality over avoidance, she decided to make herself a strong cup of coffee instead, which she sipped on while munching on the bag of chips she had carelessly picked up from downstairs.

"This is how you found him?" came the concerned voice of Miguel from the neighboring room.

"Yes," replied Maria, the hotel maid, with a hint of anxiety in her voice.

"And nobody saw what happened?" he pressed for more information.

"No, I just came in here to retrieve my phone that I left in here yesterday, and then I was met with this horrifying scene."

It must have been in that moment when he took out his phone and called the police, as she could overhear him saying, "This is Miguel calling from the Universales Hotel. We have a body with its head severed from it. It is one of my handymen; can you send someone over right away?"

In less than five minutes, Rena heard the distant wail of sirens from the approaching police vehicles. It sounded like at least half a dozen of them rushing to the scene. Suddenly, there was a determined knock on her door, and she found herself contemplating whether she should simply ignore it. However, curiosity got the better of her, and against her better judgment, she approached the door to open it.

"Hi," Miguel said, glancing over her shoulder. "I was wondering if you heard anything unusual going on in the other room?"

"No, I spent most of my time in the bathroom since it is honestly the quietest place in here. When I'm in there, I can't hear a single thing," she replied, her voice laced with a hint of concern.

"Okay," he said as he turned and walked away.

"What's going on?"

Miguel stopped and looked at her, contemplating whether he should share the grim news.

"One of our handymen got his head chopped off just a minute ago."

"Oh my God! Here, in this very building?" she gasped, her eyes widening in shock.

"Don't feel afraid; we're going to put another camera in this area soon. Rest assured, this will not happen again," he assured her, trying to maintain a calm demeanor.

"But how did this unimaginable thing happen?"

"We're still looking into the details," he replied, his tone serious as he walked away.

Rena watched his back as he moved further down the corridor and ultimately disappeared into the room next to hers. A few guests and staff members were gathered in the hallway, their eyes filled with a mix of curiosity and fear. She wasn't interested in their intrigued gazes, so she quickly escaped back into her room, closing the door firmly behind her while worrying about the manager's situation. Would this horrific incident affect his business? He was barely treading water as it was, especially with someone here capitalizing on the hotel for a prostitution ring.

She already knew it was not him. The hotel was far too quiet when he was present.

Surprisingly, he didn't appear to fit the typical mold of someone commanding attention. He was a quiet, somewhat short man endowed with large feet and an undeniably calming personality. His gentle presence made him incredibly approachable, making people feel at ease in his company. She couldn't quite comprehend why she was feeling so inexplicably nervous about their first meeting. Regardless of his mild and gentle demeanor, his attitude somehow commanded respect in a way that was both subtle and profound.

She could hear the soft murmur of the crowd gathering in the hallway, coupled with the hurried footsteps of the approaching officers. They paused at the entrance to the room where the lifeless body lay. The echoes of their chattering seemed to invade her thoughts as if they were right there beside her.

Police officers. She had never been a huge fan of them. In her experience, they epitomized the worst kind of creatures—not just in one location, but rather a uniform type that seemed to exist everywhere. She considered herself a murderess. Something otherworldly was swelling inside her, and she reveled in it. The fear that she would typically feel had evaporated, replaced instead by a thrill of excitement and temptation that thrilled her veins. However, she possessed just enough common sense to know that she needed to remain calm—to keep her cool amidst the chaos.

It was after seven in the morning when Rena gracefully walked into her small bathroom. She felt an unusual sense of calm wash over her. She was certain that she could manage whatever challenges lay ahead.

Rena went to remove the bedding that lay discarded on the bathroom floor but decided against it, just in case the officers wanted to take a closer look. Instead, she opted to engage in yoga breathing exercises for about ten minutes before the knock rang out on the door. The wave of calm that stole over her felt unnaturally strange, almost like an otherworldly embrace.

She approached the door with a mix of curiosity and apprehension. The three police officers standing there looked genuinely surprised at her unexpected appearance. Perhaps they never envisioned someone like her would be the one to answer the door. Maybe they had never encountered a black woman who presented herself in such a distinctive way.

She was dressed in a striking black scarf artfully tied around her hips and a vibrant yellow t-shirt that complemented her unique style. Her long dreadlocks cascaded down to her waist, adding to her distinctive look, while her bare feet gave her an air of casual comfort. To their eyes, she seemed like a figure transported straight from an African landscape, embodying a striking beauty that caught them off guard. She offered them a smile—not the serene, beatific smile that her sister Lena had bestowed upon her earlier, but one that still held a certain captivating charm that intrigued them. From the corner of her vision, she noticed Miguel lingering nearby, but she chose to ignore him.

One of the policemen broke the tension by asking, "Have you heard any noises coming from the room next to you?"

Rena glanced at Miguel; he was well aware of her non-existent Spanish skills, and she raised her eyebrows at him, silently urging him to help her.

He stepped forward to translate the inquiry, which was the same question he had posed earlier.

"No, I was in the bathroom. That's where I spent most of my time because it's the quietest place in here. When I'm in there I can't hear anything," she repeated the exact answer she had provided him moments before, hoping they would understand her predicament clearly.

"Can we come in and take a look?" one of the officers requested, his tone professional but inquisitive.

"Yes, sure," Rena replied after Miguel had translated. She stepped aside gracefully to allow the three policemen to enter her room, feeling a sense of relief that she had the foresight to leave her bed unmade in the bathroom. It would serve as confirmation of her truthful account.

They looked around the dimly lit space, carefully noting the haphazard placement of the suitcases behind the door, then proceeded to the cramped bathroom. Their eyes landed on the makeshift bed sprawled out on the floor, which had her MacBook Pro computer perched atop it, along with her two phones lying haphazardly, the used towel she had spread over the toilet, and an empty cup resting on a small, worn cutting board. Scattered across the makeshift bed were notebooks filled with her thoughts and a couple of well-worn novels that hinted at her late-night reading habit.

"Go into the next room, close the door, and make a loud noise," instructed the policeman, directing the other two officers with a tone that left no room for discussion.

Rena was busy folding up her bed carefully while the two were leaving the tight space. She felt a twinge of anxiety, worried he would walk all over the carefully arranged linens with his grimy shoes. Looking up from her task, she was startled to see that the policeman had stepped into the bathroom with her, closing the door firmly behind him.

As her thoughts wandered back to her sister's warning about trusting strangers, his phone suddenly rang out, slicing through the tension.

"No, nothing. Try again," he said, sounding frustrated. His phone rang a second time, and he repeated himself, "No, nothing. Okay, thanks."

The policeman glanced at her briefly before opening the bathroom door and stepping back out. Miguel was already in the room when the two policemen returned, and Rena couldn't shake the feeling that the space felt even smaller with all of them packed in there. Despite her swirling thoughts,

Rena kept her composure, praying earnestly for only one thing—a positive outcome.

Another distant siren sounded in the background, and Rena instinctively knew it was the ambulance. After they exited her room, she finished folding up her sheets with a sense of urgency and methodically put away her other belongings in their proper places. It took less than fifteen minutes for her bathroom to appear as it should again, transformed from chaos back into a normal bathroom space.

By eight-thirty in the morning, she was thoroughly bathed and dressed for the formal engagement at the embassy. She couldn't wait to finally escape the confines of the hotel. The recent death of a person had been disconcerting, to say the least. However, to her, the handyman's death felt strangely deserving; he was a bad man who needed to be vanquished from their lives. Ultimately, he suffered the consequences of his own actions.

As she walked out of her hotel room and into the bustling hallway, she noticed it was gradually getting more crowded with guests and staff alike.

"I have to go to the Jamaican embassy," she informed Miguel as she smoothly passed him by.

The embassy had been his suggestion when she found herself in his office brainstorming about the troubling issue of her expired passport. Now that she finally had the money to cover the renewal expenses, she could hardly contain her excitement at the thought of seeing her new passport.

Inside the hotel, not everyone was wearing a mask; however, to board the bus or the train, wearing a mask was strictly mandatory. She took the bus from the hotel to the Bus Terminal located on Paseo De La Reforma. From there, it was almost a two-hour drive to the closest point to her destination, and then she would still have to walk another forty-five minutes to reach the embassy itself.

The Jamaican Embassy in Mexico City was impressively Boujie. Rena had no way of knowing what to expect when they opened the elegant gates to welcome her inside. Nevertheless, she certainly wasn't expecting this level of grandeur and sophistication. There was a large, striking painting of the Prime Minister, Andrew Holmes, prominently displayed. He looked undeniably regal as he presided over the mantle of the fireplace, giving the room an air of authority. There were various rooms that served as offices throughout the Embassy. They guided her into a spacious, tastefully decorated conference room where they kindly offered her a choice of coffee or water. She opted for the refreshing water, eager to stay hydrated during her visit.

The young Jamaican man who introduced himself as Mark left the room and returned less than five minutes later with a bottle of spring water and some papers. He asked her for her birth certificate, a

Jamaican TIN number, two passport-sized pictures, her expired passport, and the processing fee. She handed him all the requested items. He carefully reviewed the documents, gave her a quick once-over, nodded his head, and then handed the papers back to her.

"Fill these out while I go and make a copy of these," he instructed.

She nodded and took the papers, which turned out to be passport forms. Picking up one of the pens on the table, she began filling in the answers to the questions. Once she had completed the forms, she put the pen and papers down.

The background music of the Jamaican orchestra added to the classy atmosphere of the room. She smiled and snuggled into the comfortable chair, taking in her surroundings. On the walls of the conference room, she noticed traditional paintings of the seven national heroes, as well as all the past Prime Ministers and the duration of their respective reigns. These paintings were hung high on the walls around the room. On the wall behind her, there were smaller paintings, each telling a different story, yet all seeming to come together when viewed as a whole.

When Mark returned, she was standing in front of a very peculiar-looking painting that seemed strikingly familiar to her, evoking a sense of déjà vu. "Where have I seen this painting before?" she wondered aloud. "I know this painting, but I can't quite remember from where," she said to him, her brows furrowed in concentration.

"You can't possibly know this painting; it was created by a man who wishes to remain anonymous. A private artist who generously donated this extraordinary piece to us. It is the only one of its kind in existence, and we have not made any replicas," he explained, his tone firm yet informative.

"Hmm." Rena pursed her lips thoughtfully and then walked away from the bothersome painting that seemed to loom over her. The unsettling image of herself, sleepwalking in the background of the artwork, struck her as a bit ominous and disturbing. Fortunately, Mark didn't seem to notice the eerie resemblance.

She moved with grace, her hands folded across her bosom, a stylish bag slung over her shoulders, and her long hair trailing behind her like a waterfall of rope wool. She presented a picture of elegance and cultural beauty, a stark contrast to the bustling atmosphere Mark had yet to fully appreciate in Mexico City. Suddenly, he felt a wave of nostalgia for his homeland wash over him.

Walking purposefully toward the table, he gathered the papers that she had left there in a disorganized stack. After meticulously making sure that all the documents were filled out properly, he reached out his hand to her with a gentle smile. "This is for you," he said.

The Jamaican

It was a receipt for the items he had received from her earlier, a token of their transaction. She walked back to the table, her movements fluid, and took the paper from him with a gracious nod.

"Your passport will be ready in three weeks. We will send you an email when it's time for you to come in and collect it."

"Thank you." She nodded her head appreciatively, feeling a wave of relief wash over her. He then escorted her to the gate, where they stood for a moment to chat about the weather and their shared experiences.

"The sun is coming out," she said, glancing up into the sun's brilliant rays and thinking of the cheerful birds that flitted through the trees nearby. She then looked around the meticulously manicured lawn and was genuinely impressed by its beauty. "This is a really nice place you guys have here."

"Yeah, but it's too small for our needs. We are currently in the process of relocating to a larger space."

"Well, I truly hope wherever you end up will be even nicer than this lovely spot."

He smiled warmly at her words, and she waved him a goodbye before proceeding through the gate, feeling grateful for their pleasant interaction.

Chapter 17
THE TRAINING

Rena didn't feel like walking the forty-five minutes to the bus stop, just yet. She had noticed a few charming restaurants on her way to the embassy and, after much consideration, decided to try the best looking one she had seen. Entering the establishment, she was greeted by the enticing aroma of delicious food, and her stomach began to protest as it cried out for nourishment. It was lunchtime, a little after twelve, and the restaurant was already packed—a promising sign to Rena that the food here must be extraordinarily good. As she stood there, contemplating her next move, an usher approached her with a welcoming smile.

"Table for how many?"

"Table for one," she replied, feeling a bit shy but undeterred.

The usher gestured for her to follow, guiding her to a small table with two chairs nestled in a cozy corner by the window. It was a pleasant spot, and she approved of the ambiance.

"As soon as a waiter is free, someone will be over," the usher assured her with a nod.

"Okay, no problem," Rena responded, settling into her seat and eagerly anticipating her meal.

Rena looked around the posh restaurant and noticed that most of the customers were elegantly well-dressed, exuding sophistication and style. She felt a sense of relief and gratitude that she had taken the time to put some extra effort into her dressing and grooming this morning. She was wearing a beautiful, flowing ankle-length white floral dress that billowed gently as she moved. Her hair, neatly tied at the nape of her neck in a sleek ponytail, showcased her delicate features. Although she usually preferred to forgo chains and necklaces, today she had decided to wear her favorite diamond stud earrings that sparkled subtly in the soft light, paired with a carefully crafted handmade bracelet given to her by a kind Pakistani man almost two years ago. The bracelet complemented her handmade leather strap slippers and matching bag perfectly, creating a cohesive look that embodied her unique personal style.

A few of the diners were discreetly casting glances in her direction, but she was accustomed to people looking her way. Looking out of the window, she took a moment to watch the passing cars darting by before her gaze was drawn to a familiar bird that caught her attention. She peered again, and sure enough, Sheel was perched gracefully on a tree branch, clearly watching her.

"Well, well. I have a guardian angel today," Rena mused softly, looking up into the sky. Although the clouds hung low, the sun broke through, shining brilliantly on everything, casting a warm glow around her. She turned to see if she could open the window, noticing that there was nothing indicating that she shouldn't. Just then, Sheel took flight, gliding effortlessly to the shrub below the window sill, where she perched calmly, intently observing her neighbors.

The approaching waitress, wearing a protective mask, looked disapprovingly at the opened window, but didn't vocalize her concerns.

"You don't mind me opening the window, do you?" Rena asked her, attempting to gauge her reaction.

"Not really, but sometimes the flies come in. Customers don't always appreciate having flies buzzing around," she replied.

"Oh." Rena had never really given much thought to the presence of flies. "Okay then, I won't order anything that is likely to attract them."

"It's really no trouble; I will go grab the netting we usually put up for the customers," the waitress assured her. She left and quickly returned a few minutes later with a crisp, white bug net that took her only a minute to expertly install. Once she was finished with the netting, she took Rena's order. Rena ordered three of the most delicious and pricey meals on the menu, including a decadent dessert. Whatever she couldn't consume at the moment, she planned to have them box it up for later, ensuring she made the most of the culinary experience. She made sure to specify that the meals should be served steaming hot.

While she waited eagerly for her meal, she tried her best to remain firmly in the present. She did not want to let her thoughts wander back to the hotel and all its memories. Suddenly, she found herself on her phone, absentmindedly Googling Kensington Avenue, Buffalo, before she could stop herself from diving into those potentially troubling thoughts.

The gruesome and shocking murder of the two male lovers was, without a doubt, the number one search topic trending across various platforms. This heinous crime not only baffled investigators but also captivated the public's attention. There was absolutely no sign of breaking and entering; in fact, even their room door appeared completely undisturbed, yet the bloody mess left behind was undeniable evidence that someone had been there. The crime scene became a significant distraction from the ongoing COVID-19 pandemic, diverting the public's focus. More and more people wrote in to express their feelings, stating that the two victims were nasty individuals who, in their opinion, deserved to die—over and over again. Many believed they had caused untold pain and suffering to both men and women, leading to a widespread sense of relief at their departure from the world. Some even went so far as to comment that they were praying for COVID-19 to take them instead. After discovering that their manhood had been so brutally involved in the crime scene, a disturbing sense of satisfaction washed over some in the community regarding whoever committed such an act. She, also, went on TikTok and found that many shared the same sentiments. Well, at least they were all in agreement with her thoughts.

The monster lurking within her was, in fact, satisfied; a small smile crept across her face, filled with a sense of twisted joy. When her meal arrived, she devoured most of it hungrily and with a sense of delight. In her own little world, she remained blissfully unaware of the curious and judgmental looks others were giving her. Such a small woman consuming all that food left them questioning: where did it all go? While her dessert was eventually boxed up for later, everything else she had consumed was gone without a trace.

She sipped her tea slowly, savoring the warmth of the cup in her hands, not wanting to think about the hotel and all that it represented. She had been there much longer than she had originally planned, and now she felt a deep yearning to leave. As she reflected on her time spent there, she realized she was going to miss her friends more than she would miss anyone else in her life. The bond she felt with them was overwhelming, a connection so profound that it was difficult for her to fully comprehend. Suddenly, an arriving email prompted her to grab her phone with a sense of urgency. It was from Kenya, the church sister whose mother had thrown her out, fully aware that she had no place to go. As Rena read the sister's heartfelt apology, something within her began to shift. Kenya's concern for the woman they had cast aside, however, felt insincere and hollow, lacking the authenticity she wished to see. Rena glanced at the email again, but then chose to ignore its presence. She could feel the falseness of their guilt swirl around her, and the darker parts of her thoughts began to emerge, akin to a murderess hiding in the shadows. With a determined shake of her head, she cast those thoughts aside and redirected her focus to the present moment.

 The sudden shriek of Sheel behind the bug net pierced through her concentration. Rena's desire to return to the hotel became urgent, almost palpable. She paid for her meal, generously leaving a substantial tip for the waitress who had served her. Hailing a taxi, she instructed the driver to take her to her favorite Soriana Supermarket in Miguel Hidalgo, Chapultepec. Once her shopping was complete, she found herself laden with an abundance of bags. To her surprise, the same taxi was waiting outside the supermarket, prepared for her return journey.

"Can you please take me to the Universales Hotel?" she firmly instructed the driver without a moment's hesitation, her voice leaving no room for doubt. It took him less than ten minutes to navigate the busy streets and arrive at their destination, and he charged her the correct fee without any fuss. She was pleasantly surprised when he offered to help her carry her things up to her room, a gesture of kindness that she graciously accepted. As she entered the hotel, she noticed the hallway was completely empty of people, which brought her a sense of relief amidst the bustling city outside. Rena attempted to tip the driver for his assistance, but he insisted on refusing the money, waving her off kindly as he left. That truly was nice of him. The very moment she set aside the last of her purchases, Tuck appeared in her room, his presence as familiar as the air she breathed.

"Did you send the driver for me?" she asked, curious about his intentions.

"Yes," he replied simply. It didn't particularly surprise her anymore. She was beginning to understand the extraordinary power they wielded within their realm.

"How long have you been living there?" Rena pointed her chin in the direction of the ancient trees outside, her curiosity piqued.

"We have been living there for almost three thousand years," he responded, his tone steady.

"And nobody notices you?" She was genuinely taken aback, a mix of intrigue and disbelief flooding through her.

"Humans are surprisingly blind when it comes to perceiving otherworldly beings. Throughout history, countless entities and spirits have passed through their realm, yet they never seemed to notice a thing." He quickly changed the subject, as if he were in a hurry to impart essential knowledge to her. "Your training will primarily focus on self-control. Specifically, it will teach you how to master your inner being when it desperately wants to break free and manifest itself. The stronger you become in your abilities, the more that inner force will desire to rear its head and assert its dominance."

She found that notion believable.

"In order to control it effectively, you must not give in to its demands at whim. For instance, today you managed exceptionally well after reading that email."

Rena was taken aback. "How did you know that?" "I know everything, little one. Everything," he said, meeting her gaze.

She understood he was referring to the incident in Buffalo, but she pursed her lips, refusing to show any emotion, and looked straight ahead at the other pretentious trees surrounding them.

"The very moment you start allowing it to take over, is the precise moment you will begin losing your sense of self. The only way to prevent that from happening is to effectively seal it off."

"Seal it off? How can I possibly do that? Isn't it an inherent part of me?"

"Yes, it is indeed a part of you, but crucially, it is not the entirety of who you are."

"But how exactly do I seal it off?"

"Yo...!"

He didn't get the chance to finish his sentence. Ananuyah and Lena suddenly appeared before him, interrupting the tension that had filled the air.

"I fucking told you he was going to try to disarm her," Lena exclaimed, her voice laced with urgency as she vanished the other trees in their path before reaching for her gleaming golden sword.

"Stop, Lena! You can't hurt your father!" Ananuyah shouted desperately, trying to intervene.

"What the fuck!!" both Lena and Rena shouted simultaneously, their voices echoing in disbelief.

Tuck looked resigned, understanding dawning on him. He had suspected this twist in the unfolding drama when the flickering woman had come to her rescue, but he hadn't been entirely certain. It was only after he rushed to save her and caught a whiff of her unique earthy scent that his suspicions were fully realized and confirmed.

~~~~~~~

Rena couldn't believe what she was hearing. She was a monster who thrived on the pain of others and derived twisted pleasure from their suffering. To make matters even more bizarre, her father was an ancient tree, standing tall and proud, who had existed for over three thousand long years. Meanwhile, her mother and twin sister resided in an entirely different dimension, wielding extraordinary powers, and they had a… Rena abruptly stopped her swirling thoughts and turned her gaze to Ananuyah, her heart racing.

"And what is your purpose here? Who exactly are you?"

"I am your grandmother, and I have been alive for over fifty thousand years," Ananuyah replied with an air of certainty.

"What?!!" Rena and Lena, her sister, exclaimed in unison, both equally shocked by the revelation.

It seemed Lena was just as much in the dark about this perplexing family history as Rena was.

"*I am not merely three thousand years old, little one. I live as a magnificent tree for three thousand years*," he corrected her, his deep voice resonating with wisdom.

"Let me regurgitate all of this information," Rena said, firmly shutting them off to process this new reality. Just then, a sharp knock echoed through her door. With relief, she walked to the entrance, eager for a distraction. Miguel stood there, looking concerned yet familiar.

"Please come in," she warmly invited, knowing that he would be oblivious to the extraordinary guests in her room.

"Oh, you have guests?" he remarked, instantly proving her wrong and leaving Rena feeling a swirl of confusion.

"You can see them?" Rena was astounded and taken aback by the unexpected revelation.

"Miguel is my son," Tuck interjected, a hint of pride in his voice. "He has been looking out for you at my request, ever since this all began."

This was too much for Rena to comprehend. Unable to contain herself any longer, she bursted out laughing.

"What's next? The dead tree across the road is your tree carcass and my mother didn't really disappear; she turned into a tree, too? This is just outrageous!"

Rena was on the verge of walking out when Ananuyah softly spoke up.

"Actually, you are correct about one thing regarding the tree carcass. It belongs to Miguel, but your mother didn't turn into a tree. We are still actively searching for her."

Rena looked around at them all, feeling a swirl of emotions, and couldn't help but sense a conspiracy brewing beneath the surface.

~~~~~~

"The camera picked up a man going into the room next door, accompanied by the handyman, but unfortunately, the footage only captured him exiting. The police are currently suspecting foul play." Miguel, her new brother, told the room, glancing at her briefly before he turned his gaze to Lena and the others, who were still present in the room, before making his way out.

"I'm so tired!" she announced to the others in a dismissive tone, hoping they would understand her need for solitude.

Lena carefully returned the trees to their proper place before quietly fizzling out of existence. At that moment, Ananuyah and Tuck exited simultaneously as well. Rena then walked over to the window to draw the curtains, not wanting to see anyone at the moment, her heart heavy with exhaustion.

The clock on the side table read five-fifteen when she finally laid down. Her tiredness felt profound and overwhelming, weighing her down. She was convinced that if she fell asleep right now, something would inevitably attract unwanted attention.

Feeling restless, she got up and rummaged through her bag to find the red cinnamon candle she had purchased at the cozy little candle store near the restaurant. She lit it, placing it carefully on the candle holder she had bought specifically for this purpose. Just as Rena was about to climb back into bed, she realized she was still wearing her street clothes, which she found uncomfortable. She got up again, to find something more suitable, and wiped down her body before putting on the long, soft house dress and a pair of cozy socks.

She was climbing back into bed when her Zelle notification pinged. It was Luke, depositing another five hundred dollars into her account.

"He better keep that shit coming," she muttered with a wicked grin, feeling a mix of irritation and appreciation.

"THE TREES MAY NOT HAVE EYES LIKE US, BUT THEY'RE SEEING EVERYTHING, EVEN THE DUST."

"THE TREES MAY NOT HAVE EARS LIKE US, BUT THEY'RE LISTENING TO EVERYTHING, EVEN WHEN WE FIGHT AND CUSS."

"THE TREES MAY NOT HAVE MOUTH LIKE US, BUT THEY EAT, SPEAK AND NEVER MAKE FUSS."

"THE TREES MAY NOT HAVE FEET LIKE US, BUT THEY'RE WALKING, EVEN WHILE YOU CATCH THE BUS."

Chapter 18
HER MONSTER

One week straight, Rena had lived in the hotel, completely free from any disturbance of any kind that might disrupt her fragile peace. She had not returned to the bathroom to sleep since the fateful day of the horrifying discovery of the handyman's unfortunate fate. Additionally, Miguel had successfully managed to keep most of the other guests confined to the other sides of the hotel, which provided her the much-needed quiet she desperately craved.

With him being there, coupled with their gnawing fear of being murdered, those individuals who had been involved in using the hotel for their unnatural purposes were now keeping an unusually low profile. It certainly helped that Miguel remained on-site to keep a vigilant eye on things. However, she suspected that it was the intriguing nature she represented, along with the revelation of their complicated relationship, that played a significant role in their caution. Perhaps, just like the others, he was endeavoring to help keep her calm in her turbulent state. She grappled with the reality that she had become a monster, a creature who took pleasure in murder.

The thought was becoming painfully repetitive, and so was her incessant struggle to keep the monster within her firmly in check. She was utterly exhausted by it all. Rena also noticed that, remarkably, this past week was the first time in her entire life that she had experienced such a long stretch without any form of visitation. Surrounded by powerful beings, it was, of course, only natural that they would ensure she remained undisturbed during this tumultuous time.

She had no pressing need to step outside the confines of her cozy hotel room. With an ample supply of food available, she could easily sustain herself comfortably for a good two weeks without venturing out into the bustling world beyond her door.

Each day passed in a haze of eating, sleeping, watching lengthy YouTube videos, and immersing herself in the pages of various books. Yet, as time went on, her thoughts drifted back to the fact that her books were still not selling, leaving her perplexed and wondering, why was that? During her stay at the hotel, she had poured her heart into writing another book, but, like her previous works, it too seemed destined to rest in the online garbage pile of Amazon's vast marketplace.

"Who was actually responsible for book sales on Amazon, anyway?" She mused, a hint of frustration creeping into her thoughts. She had cultivated grand ambitions, and with those lofty dreams came the essential need for money. Deep down, she firmly believed that her books were of a caliber capable of bringing in a substantial income, and she knew that without a doubt.

Just then, another five hundred dollars came in from Luke; he had been unwaveringly sending it to her every single day at the same time, like clockwork. She could almost visualize him behind the scenes, calculating and raising his prices, all because of her.

Rena vividly remembered his earnest prayer to Jesus, a heartfelt promise that he would finally stop selling illegal drugs. But in truth, he could never truly stop. This lifeline was the only thing that was propelling him towards wealth, and he absolutely reveled in the idea of being rich. As thoughts of her own financial struggles stirred restlessly, the monster began to rear its ugly head. She quickly redirected her thoughts.

Who, she wondered, was actually responsible for the sales of books on Amazon? She found herself perusing some particularly disappointing books authored by specific groups, which only served to amplify her growing irritation. Finally taking action, she reached for her phone to conduct some research, a sense of anticipation fluttering within her. But in a sudden moment of indecision, she dropped the phone and decided instead to retrieve a Snickers bar from the sizable stash she had purchased earlier. They had been much cheaper at the supermarket than at the shop downstairs, a small victory that brought her a faint sense of satisfaction. With each satisfying bite, she felt herself gradually calming, the sweet chocolate melting away her worries ever so slightly.

    Rena was diligently teaching herself how to control her emotions, a challenging task that seemed to require endless patience and focus. She understood that mastering her emotions and thoughts was akin to asserting control over the monstrous presence that lurked within her. Her tumultuous thoughts and deeply felt emotions were intricately connected to that inner beast. Yet, she couldn't shake the nagging realization that she was human; how was she going to navigate her life as a human being without the innate ability to express her emotions freely? After all, humans are inherently emotional creatures, driven by their feelings and desires.

    She pursed her lips thoughtfully, then picked up her phone and quickly googled, "who's in charge of Amazon publishing?" As the search results appeared, she noted the headquarters were located in Seattle, Washington. She discovered that some key individuals, including publisher Miyala Bruder and publisher David Klum, were prominently involved in the operation.

    Hmm, maybe she should consider giving them a visit to pitch her ideas. The monster inside her perked up at the thought of such a bold move. No, she thought, there surely must be a more effective way for her books to gain the visibility they deserved.

Suddenly, Rena realized she was missing the comfortable bathroom floor beneath her. She got up and decided to unmake her bed. Gathering most of the bedding, she carried it into the bathroom and made a makeshift bed on the floor, covering the toilet seat with a plush towel to create a small haven. With that task accomplished, she returned to retrieve her computer, other books, notes, and even her washbasin.

Satisfied that everything was arranged just as it should be, she ventured out to grab a bottle of water and some chips to snack on while she indulged in some casual YouTube browsing.

Her time at the hotel was swiftly coming to an end, she could feel it in the pit of her stomach. But where would she go next? The crisp chill of late December surrounded her, marking nearly a year and some weeks since she had first arrived in vibrant Mexico City. What was her next move in this unpredictable journey? Rena fell asleep that night with many pressing questions swirling in her mind, each one intertwined with her hopes and uncertainties about her future.

Waking up in a state of confusion, she noted with surprise that she was no longer in her familiar hotel room. Instead, she found herself in Kenys's large apartment situated on Miguel Hidalgo. Rena stood in the girl's bedroom, observing the peaceful scene before her; the girl was fast asleep, curled snugly against her fiancé. Rena couldn't help but feel a surge of disdain, aware that they were engaging in intimate activities while pretending to be holier than thou when they were attending church services together. With a heavy heart, she looked at them one last time before walking out and stepping into the adjacent bedroom, where the mother lay sleeping soundly with her little chihuahua nestled closely in front of her, and her cat lounging comfortably behind her.

    The cat, noticing Rena's presence, lifted her black and white furry head and let out a curious meow. Rena approached the cat and gently stroked her soft head in a moment of tenderness. However, her demeanor shifted as she then bent low to seize the mother by the throat with a swift and decisive grip. The terrified woman's face turned an alarming shade of blue, her legs flapping helplessly as her hands instinctively clutched at her throat, desperately trying to free it from the invisible hand that was constricting her airways. Her wide, frightened eyes darted around in a panic, searching for the entity that was holding her captive. Except for the streetlight outside, which did not quite reach the dimly lit rooftop bedroom, she was unable to see anything at all. Rena then walked to the window, carrying the flailing woman with ease, as though she were no more substantial than a mere paperweight. With a swift motion, she opened the window and placed the terrified woman on the windowsill, finally relinquishing her death grip on her throat. The woman inhaled sharply, gasping for air as she clutched her throat and struggled to steady herself.

Kenya and her mother lived together on the top floor of their impressive four-storey building. This beautifully designed structure was lovingly owned and maintained by their family for many years.

Suddenly, the piercing sound of a dog barking abruptly shattered the peaceful quiet of the night, cutting through the stillness like a knife. Rena could distinctively hear the hurried footsteps of the two fornicators approaching quickly.

"Mama! What are you doing?" Kenya exclaimed in alarm as her eyes fell upon her mother precariously balancing on the windowsill. Pedro, her startled fiancé, was rendered speechless, his body frozen in shock at the shocking sight before him.

In a frantic moment, Rena pushed the mother off the windowsill, disregarding the screams of the two. She watched intently as the woman went crashing down onto the pavement of the sidewalk below. Her unfortunate landing involved a grim surprise as her face met the pile of dog waste that she had failed to pick up during her evening stroll earlier with the dog.

Feeling a twisted sense of satisfaction, Rena stepped aside from the chaos unfolding around her.

"No Mama! Why?" Kenya cried out desperately, rushing past her in a panic as she grabbed the keys awkwardly. In her frantic urgency to reach her mother, she neglected to realize that she was inappropriately dressed for the late hour. However, Pedro had noticed this detail and hurriedly moved to retrieve her robe just as he was collecting his own garments.

Rena stood still for a moment, her eyes fixed on the sorrowful couple who were kneeling over the woman they affectionately called Mama. The scene before her was heart-wrenching, and a strange sense of satisfaction washed over her, a feeling that was both unsettling and strangely comforting. Without a word, she turned and vanished into the shadows, leaving behind the weight of their grief.

As dawn broke, Rena woke up at six in the early morning, the sun just beginning to peek over the horizon. It was Saturday, a day that promised adventure and exploration, the perfect opportunity to visit some of the intriguing places in the city she had not yet had the chance to discover. Stretching her arms and yawning softly, she fleetingly thought about the church sister, her expression tinged with annoyance.

"Hmm," she mused to herself, reflecting on how she hated regrets. A firm resolve settled in her mind — she was not going to dwell on what had transpired the night before.

Her vessel felt cold against the chilly morning air, a stark reminder of the brisk weather outside. She instinctively pulled up the thick, cozy blanket that Maria had given her two weeks ago, just after the weather channel had warned of a sudden cold front sweeping through the city. Suddenly, her vessel began to itch, a distraction that pulled her from her thoughts and reminded her of the need to address the little discomforts that nagged at her.

Looking up, she noticed with a sense of surprise that the window was wide open. She must have forgotten to close it securely last night before drifting off to sleep. With a soft sigh, she got up, wrapping the warm blanket snugly around her shoulders for comfort. She was so accustomed to glancing over at her frie—family—that the action felt entirely instinctual, performed without the slightest bit of thought. Suddenly, Rena noticed a flash of light near Sarai and her expression shifted to one of concern. Without hesitation, she raced into her room, hurrying to the larger window, and quickly removed the curtains to get a better view. There stood the owner of the building, nonchalantly smoking a cigarette while trying to peer into Sarai's room. A wave of relief washed over her as she recognized he was harmless. She promptly closed the curtains and made her way back to the bathroom, ensuring she shut the window firmly before returning to her cozy bed.

A few places in the neighborhood were starting to open their doors, even though COVID-19 was still raging throughout Mexico, creating an atmosphere of uncertainty. Business had to go on; people needed to earn their living to survive.

Rena was becoming increasingly restless. The wanderlust that often gripped her was overwhelming her once again, but she had to remind herself that she still had another week to wait before her passport would finally arrive. As she gazed at the rising sun, her mind swirled with thoughts of what she might do today. She considered the ambitious new book she had just started writing, but instead of excitement, she felt a wave of discouragement wash over her. What's the use in writing if nobody was reading? A sense of hopelessness threatened to overtake her, but then she quickly shifted her thoughts. There's so much beauty to see here, she reminded herself, trying to chase away the negative feelings that loomed.

There's money safely tucked into your account, and she had also managed to find a weird family, as well. All these years, she had genuinely wondered about her elusive father and now, surprisingly, she had learnt that he was a tree. The thought made her want to laugh hard. How on earth did they even meet, anyway? Her mother, a vibrant Jamaican woman, and her father, an extraordinary Mexican tree. Her entire body shook with the absurdity of it all, and laughter bubbled up inside her. Growing up, she had always been curious and questioned her father's absence, but her aunt didn't know anything, and she couldn't tell her what she didn't know. Now, here she was, coincidentally living in the same neighborhood, in Mexico, with a tree for a father. The situation was just too incredulous; she held onto her belly and erupted into laughter. How was she ever going to get used to this astonishing revelation?

Rena looked over at the darkened trees and suddenly saw something quite peculiar. A large brown bird was perched on the very top of Sarai's head, staring intently at her. It was an osprey. This was the first time she had ever encountered one up so close and personal. What was it doing there, staring directly at her? She knew that the trees attracted all kinds of birds, but she couldn't remember having seen any eagles in their midst before. Suddenly, another osprey flew by, then gracefully turned around to land beside its buddy, both observing her with keen interest. This was undeniably too weird. They were both looking at her intently. But why?

Rena felt the hair rising on her back in an unsettling way. The strong, overwhelming need to escape this place was becoming increasingly stronger by the moment. After giving the birds outside another cautious glance before firmly shutting the curtain, Rena set about unmaking her bed in the bathroom, tidying her room with care, and then taking a refreshing shower before dressing for the day ahead. It was still early in the morning, but she knew there were several coffee shops opened along Paseo De La Reforma that she could explore.

As she made her way downstairs, she spotted Miguel in the receptionist area.

"Good morning, Miguel," she greeted him cheerfully, trying to mask her unease.

"Good morning to you too. Where are you headed off to so early?" he asked, looking a bit surprised.

"I'm not exactly sure yet. Do you have any recommendations?" she responded, her voice filled with curiosity.

"Where have you been since you got here?" he inquired, genuinely interested.

"Truth be told, I haven't had the chance to go anywhere much, except for the few nearby places I could walk to," she admitted.

"Well, do you mind if I accompany you? I would love to be your guide today," he offered with a warm smile, making her feel a bit more at ease.

Rena gave him a suspicious look that clearly conveyed her uncertainty. He laughed lightly, as if trying to ease her doubt.

"Actually, I've been wanting to ask you for some time now. I know you're bored stiff all by your lonesome up there in that quiet place of yours."

And truth be told, she was indeed freaking bored stiff up there, feeling the weight of isolation pressing down on her. She could definitely use some invigorating company and a break from the monotony.

"Okay," she finally decided after a moment of consideration, nodding her head in agreement.

"Good. Give me just a minute to get someone to cover for me," he replied enthusiastically.

"No problem," she assured him, feeling a hint of excitement.

Miguel brought out a sleek Mercedes Benz model that she had never seen before, its curves and shine catching her eye. Rena raised her eyebrows at him in surprise, but he pretended not to see her reaction and simply smiled.

She felt a sense of satisfaction knowing she had bought herself a simple but elegant dress for this unplanned occasion. Although it had cost her almost three hundred American dollars, she strongly believed it was well worth the investment to look her best.

As they drove, Miguel passed by a few places Rena recognized from memory. Although she had passed by them countless times, she had never really had the financial means to enjoy them the way they deserved. Suddenly, he pulled into the luxurious Hotel Marquis, a grand structure that loomed impressively. Instead of getting out and handing the key over to the concierge, he drove towards the back of the luscious garden park, navigating expertly towards a tall, high wall. Rena was utterly surprised when the imposing wall magically opened into a tunnel, and without hesitation, he entered, leaving her both bewildered and intrigued.

The tunnel was properly paved and painted a deep, glossy black, with elegant sconces lighting placed every four feet, casting a warm glow that made the journey feel almost mystical.

"Don't worry, I'm not going to kidnap you," Miguel reassured her halfway through the darkened tunnel, his voice steady and calm.

She wasn't fearful, but rather filled with a bubbling sense of anticipation as they moved deeper into the unknown.

It took a long five hours before she finally caught sight of the sun again, a brilliant orb that seemed to welcome her back to the surface. She felt an exhilarating rush, as if she were embarking on an extraordinary adventure. While Miguel skillfully maneuvered the vehicle, he passionately shared with her the true history of Mexico, a narrative far removed from the overly simplistic tales that had been regurgitated for centuries. He even delved into the enigmatic story of the Olmecs, a fascinating civilization whose disappearance was still steeped in mystery.

"My kind have been around since prehistoric times," he explained, a hint of pride in his voice. "Our unique ability to shape-shift has given us an undeniable edge over other animals, mammals, humans, and even those rare human-plant hybrids… us. When that catastrophic asteroid struck the Earth and nearly decimated our planet from the solar system, our entire species was on the brink of complete desecration, had it not been for the concealed tunnel we just navigated through, we might never have found ourselves here, alive and brimming with stories yet to unfold.

When the asteroid hit, it not only damaged the tunnel, but remarkably, the broken tunnel ultimately became a sanctuary that saved the children. Because they were in plant form, the tunnel had managed to keep three of those children safe from harm. It took them a staggering fifty years to realize they were not merely trees and another fifty to learn how to shape-shift into their original forms. During that extensive period, they spread their roots far and wide throughout Mexico and other areas of the world, leaving traces of their existence in destinies intertwined with nature."

Rena listened with rapt attention to the incredible stories he told. She had never encountered anything quite like this in her life. "How was it possible that nobody knows this side of Earth's history?" she asked, genuinely intrigued.

"Oh, a few select individuals who controlled the Earth and its economy are certainly aware. However, the biblical tales not only solidified their power, but also effectively dumbed down mankind, preventing the masses from discovering their true potentials and capabilities."

That was such a profound statement that resonated deeply with Rena. She had been told something similar when she was in university back in America, but at the time, she had dismissed it as mere propaganda. Now, here she was, receiving this powerful insight straight from the horse's mouth.

Miguel laughed heartily, his eyes sparkling with a delightful gleam of mischief.

"Yes, I used to be a horse too," he said with a playful grin.

Rena couldn't help but join in, laughing along with him. It felt incredibly good to hear the sound of her laughter echoing in the air, a pleasant reminder of the joy that often resided just out of reach. Sighing deeply, she felt as if a heavy weight had just been lifted off her shoulders, making her feel lighter and more at ease.

"Ah, so you know what's taking place in your hotel then?" she inquired.

"I always know what's going on in all my hotels," he replied, his tone serious yet laced with a hint of irony.

"So why don't you just put a stop to it?" she asked, curiosity bubbling inside her.

"What's happening in my hotel is unfortunately happening all over Mexico, and indeed, across the entire Americas and around the world," he explained in a calm yet fervent manner. "If I were to simply put a stop to it in my hotel, they would just relocate it to another venue. All of the hard work I have put into trying to root out the horrific child prostitution problems here and globally would be undone, pushing me back several years in my efforts."

This was such a shocking revelation to her. He was fully aware of what was unfolding around him, but to effectively eradicate such a deep-rooted issue from existence, he had to allow it to continue within his hotel's walls. It was akin to chopping off an arm to save the body. Suddenly, everything began to make perfect sense to her. Rena found herself looking at her newfound brother through a lens of profound understanding. He was a clever and astute individual, and she now recognized the wisdom behind his actions.

Miguel burst out laughing once more. "Thank you for that," he said, still chuckling, clearly delighted to have lifted the veil of understanding between the two of them.

"THE TREES MAY NOT HAVE EYES LIKE US, BUT THEY'RE SEEING EVERYTHING, EVEN THE DUST."

"THE TREES MAY NOT HAVE EARS LIKE US, BUT THEY'RE LISTENING TO EVERYTHING, EVEN WHEN WE FIGHT AND CUSS."

"THE TREES MAY NOT HAVE MOUTH LIKE US, BUT THEY EAT, SPEAK AND NEVER MAKE FUSS."

"THE TREES MAY NOT HAVE FEET LIKE US, BUT THEY'RE WALKING, EVEN WHILE YOU CATCH THE BUS."

Chapter 19
A NEW WORLD

Looking around in awe and sheer astonishment, Rena fully admired the bizarre and otherworldly landscape that Miguel had driven them into, each detail more astonishing than the last. It appeared somewhat like Earth, yet for some strange and inexplicable reason that was difficult to pinpoint, it didn't feel remotely like Earth at all—almost as if it were a vibrant dream plucked from the depths of her imagination.

"Where exactly are we?" she asked, her voice infused with a mix of fascination and wonder that echoed through the still, ethereal air surrounding them.

"We're in the tree dimension," Miguel replied, his eyes twinkling with a deep understanding and an undeniable sense of mystery.

"Wait, I thought Earth was the three-dimensional realm we all know and understand," Rena mentioned, taking another sweeping glance at the environment that Earth could have easily mirrored, had greed and selfishness not overtaken the hearts and minds of mankind in a profound way.

"No, not three, but rather the tree dimension. This is the very dimension you used when you were able to correspond with my father and the others," he clarified, his tone steady and reassuring, as if sharing a treasured secret.

Rena's mouth opened wide like a gasping fish, but astonishingly, nothing intelligible came out as she struggled to process the unexpected revelation unfolding before her. Miguel gave her a moment to gather herself and sort through her swirling thoughts, patiently waiting for her to find her voice once again amidst the chaos of her emotions.

"Is this, by any chance, where my mother and sister came when I was born?" She finally asked, her voice quivering slightly with a hopeful, yet anxious, anticipation that hung heavily in the air between them.

"Yes," he confirmed, his voice steady.

"But they died. How could they have died and come here?"

"Nothing actually died, Rena. When things seem to be lifeless, they merely disappear from one dimension and transition into another. Your mother and sister did not truly perish; they left their original bodies behind and arrived here in this realm where they adopted entirely new forms and readjusted to their new existence."

"So, I could leave my body in the hotel and come here to inhabit a new body, just like in the movie, The Avatar?"

Miguel felt a growing sense of exasperation with her thought process. "No, you can't simply switch dimensions like those misguided individuals are claiming. You can switch bodies, but in order for that transformation to happen, your human body has to unfortunately expire."

"I don't understand. I can only come here if I no longer have use of my human vessel?"

"Yes, that is correct."

"Then what am I doing here? Did I die?" Rena questioned, her voice tinged with panic as the unsettling realization began to sink in deeper. She was becoming increasingly alarmed, her heart racing at the thought of her existence possibly coming to an abrupt end. She liked her human body, cherished it deeply, every unique experience and sensation that came with it. She found profound joy in the vibrant experiences of living on her splendid three-dimensional Earth, reveling in the warmth of the sun and the sound of laughter around her. Her vessel couldn't possibly be compromised—not when she felt so incredibly alive and full of potential.

"No, you're not dead. You came through the tunnel," he explained calmly. "Engaging in that journey allows you to visit the tree dimension without facing any dire consequences."

In that moment, it totally made sense to her. The tunnel represented the woman's womb, a powerful and sacred gateway of life. Man can only enter Earth through the sacred female passage, she thought, marveling at the deep intricacies of existence. The tree dimension, too, had a remarkably similar concept that fascinated her beyond words.

"Ahh!" She shouted out in surprise and wonder. "So Earth has a tunnel like this that allows beings from other dimensions to enter?"

"Yes, indeed. Anything that's not of Earth must embark on a journey through a mystical tunnel in order to enter her truly magnificent and extraordinary realm. Those aliens who possess the remarkable ability to appear and disappear at will also had to traverse the same enigmatic tunnel," he clarified patiently, his voice steady and reassuring, infused with a sense of wisdom.

"But what about Ananuyah and my sister? How exactly are they able to move around freely?"

"They are more than mere one-dimensional creatures, encompassing you as well. Since you exist in both this dimension and that other one, it means you can come and go at will, but only if you relinquish your earthly avatar, just like the others. Alternatively, if you choose to retain your physical vessel, you can still arrive here by way of the tunnel."

Rena processed that information thoughtfully for a moment while letting her gaze wander around the surroundings. There were indeed many humans present here, she noted with curiosity. She began to suspect that they were the enigmatic descendants of the Olmec civilization that had mysteriously disappeared from the face of the earth—her suspicions strengthened by their striking resemblance.

It was undeniably strange the way she was witnessing them shape-shifting in and out of both human and tree form, just like Tuck had done so effortlessly on the rooftop. She observed several shape-shifters moving fluidly between their human forms and breathtaking dinosaur shapes. Rena also noticed quite a few majestic mammoths slowly roaming the area, their colossal silhouettes casting shadows on the ground. The sight of these extraordinary prehistoric images was so shocking and surreal that she could feel her entire being instinctively going into attack mode.

Miguel, ever observant, noted the significant change in her energy field and quickly held up his hands in a calming gesture.

"They are just shape-shifters, Rena. They won't harm you," he reassured her.

The urgent need to process all of this overwhelming information was so great that Rena scanned her surroundings, searching desperately for somewhere to sit down and gather her thoughts.

"Is there somewhere I can go to freshen up?" she asked quietly, feeling the need to escape the intensity of the moment.

"Sure," he replied, gesturing to an opening beside them that she had somehow overlooked amidst her chaotic thoughts and feelings. They entered a brick building that resembled the Hotel Marquis they had previously entered to get to the tunnel. Miguel kindly showed her to a cozy room, explaining that this would be her space for the duration of her visit.

It was a very large and beautifully designed living room, tastefully decorated in a modern style, with lush green plants adorning every corner. She entered a grand master bedroom and suddenly realized she was in the master suite of an extremely luxurious hotel. It was the most opulent luxury she had ever experienced in her life. This extravagant ambiance changed her mood completely, wrapping her in a sense of comfort and serenity. The bathroom, as she explored, was encased entirely in glass, cleverly blanketed by foliage so thick that no one could see her through them, creating an intimate sanctuary.

It was very quiet. A calmness that felt strikingly similar to Miguel's tranquil demeanor when he was at the hotel enveloped her, stealing over her like a warm, gentle wave.

"Okay! Who's there?" she asserted, putting her hands on her hips and slowly turning to see which one of her mysterious visitors would show themselves first. A small, familiar-looking shrub, whose roots seemed to grow into the flooring, shimmered softly, and then in its place stood Matilda, the sleek cat. The large ficus tree in the corner of the bathroom shook violently for a brief moment and then disappeared entirely. Ananuyah stood in its place, looking regal. Rena pursed her lips thoughtfully and walked over to the elegant bathroom sink.

"I didn't peg you for a ficus," she observed, turning on the faucet and washing her hands thoroughly.

"The ficus trees are the most ignored trees in your world. Here, they are cherished and revered," Ananuyah explained, gracefully sitting on the bathroom counter and crossing her legs with poise. She was the very picture of elegance and sophistication.

Rena didn't say anything at all; instead, she was deeply pondering who was going to transform from flowers into something else next.

"Don't worry, we are the only fake plant in your room," Ananuyah reassured her gently. Rena then wiped her hands on the towel provided for her use. When she was finally done, she noticed that the towel turned a vibrant green for just a moment, then returned to its original white color, with all the wet finger marks completely disappearing without a trace.

She looked at the towel for a few seconds, shrugged her shoulders in mild confusion, and walked out of the bathroom to rejoin the world outside.

"Everything in here is organic and specially designed; they regenerate themselves entirely after use," Ananuyah explained.

It was clear to Ananuyah that the young one was not in the mood for any kind of company, so she turned to leave.

"Thank you. I'm just not good company right now. As soon as I figure out why I'm feeling this way, I promise I'll be better company," Rena stated as a form of apology, hoping her message was received.

"No worries at all. Get some rest. We will see you later," Ananuyah said with a warm smile before disappearing into thin air, leaving Rena alone with the cat.

Rena folded her arms in thought and stared at the cat intently. "At least you could have given me some warning about all of this," she remarked, half hoping for some kind of acknowledgment from the quiet feline.

"I couldn't. Not in your world," the black feline cat replied, her voice melodious and soothing like the rush of a waterfall in the early morning.

"What the fuck! You can talk for real?" Rena exclaimed, her eyes wide with sheer astonishment as the gravity of the moment began to sink in.

The Jamaican

"Yes. And I can do this too," the cat said, a playful glint dancing in its bright eyes, before transforming into Sarai—the stunning human form that Rena had only ever dared to imagine in her wildest dreams and fantasies.

"Oh my God! This is utterly insane," Rena exclaimed, her heart racing furiously in her chest. She walked over to Sarai, her hands trembling slightly, and wrapped her arms around the exquisite female, overcome with joy and disbelief at finally meeting her in person, after all this time she had waited and wished for this encounter.

Sarai was as dark as a Sudanese, her skin radiant and mesmerizing under the ambient light of the room, and just as tall, towering with a graceful presence that commanded attention and admiration. Her startling beauty was so captivating that Rena couldn't help but stare, completely enchanted and utterly shameless in her awe. Sarai laughed, a melodic sound that rang out like sweet music, exposing her milky white teeth that perfectly complemented the rich hazel of her expressive eyes. The sight of her filled Rena with such an overwhelming sense of happiness and pure awe that it took a full minute for her to fully process what happened next in this bewildering encounter.

"I can't stay long, but someone here is absolutely dying to meet you," Sarai added, her tone laced with both urgency and excitement that hinted at deeper mysteries waiting to unfold.

Sarai barely finished her sentence when she disappeared from her surroundings, only to find another familiar-smelling male materializing before her.

"How am I able to see you?" she questioned, her curiosity piqued.

"In this unique dimension, you can indeed see me, but only in this specific form," her soul explained, with a hint of warmth in its tone.

"Are you from this dimension?" she inquired further, feeling an overwhelming urge to touch him, yet tethered by her trepidation.

"No. I hail from the twenty-fifth dimensional space-time Earth, serving as the head of the guardians for this solar system. You are able to see me now because you currently reside in the twelfth dimensional space-time Earth. Although you can't perceive the entirety of my being at this moment, rest assured that your eyesight will not be adversely affected," he clarified, a confident glint in his eyes.

His cockiness was undeniably stirring something deep within her heart. "Well, Mr. Space-time cockiness, I must say, I am beyond happy to finally see you," she told him, a broad smile spreading across her face, as she desperately wanted to reach out and bridge the gap between them.

Her body was already ablaze, engulfed in an inferno of uncontrolled sensations, and her nerve endings were on the brink of a fiery eruption. The overwhelming feelings she was unable to regulate whenever he was near her on third-dimensional earth multiplied exponentially with the number of dimensions they traversed in, plunging both her and her beast into a state of unrelenting rabid frenzy. They were spiraling into chaos. Her eyes flared to a deep crimson, and plumes of smoke billowed forth from her nostrils and ears like a dragon unleashed. In a moment of sheer instinct, Rena lunged for his throat, her fingers elongating by four inches, tipped by nails that had darkened to a sinister black. A force deep within her battled to rein in her beast, but she was far too consumed by the tempest of emotions to pay it any mind.

"You can't hurt me," he told her with unnerving calmness, raising his hands in a gesture meant to pacify the help that had rushed to his side. Jahazap, her soul and inner essence, locked his gaze with hers, leaning in closer so that he could whisper soothingly into her ear.

"You will not hurt me. I am you. You are me. We are one and the same being. We are one and the same." His body radiated an intense frost that felt like ice against her skin, and he continued to murmur gently, creating a sanctuary of calm amidst her storm. The chilling presence of his words and touch was gradually penetrating the haze of her overactive mind, awakening her to clarity. With a final, deep breath, she managed to retract her monstrous form, both trembling still as they surrendered to the slow dissipating of the heat that had consumed them moments before.

She started crying, tears streaming down her cheeks. She had grown so strong during her journey, since she had made the bold decision to embrace the darkness that resided within her, but she never expected to find herself feeling this powerful.

"There now, you're okay," he reassured her as he held her tightly while she cried her heart out, letting all her pent-up emotions flow free.

What was happening to her? Why did she suddenly lash out and attack him? What was this strange and chaotic force within her that seemed to have no rhyme or reason? She knew him well, so why had she suddenly turned rabid on him, as if she were a completely different person? Rena couldn't comprehend the turmoil that was erupting inside her.

"I don't know what just happened. I don't understand what's truly happening to me," she whispered through her sobs.

They were lying side by side on the grand king-sized bed in her temporary suite, the luxurious surroundings feeling distant and surreal. A breakfast tray lay precariously on the bed beside them, a reminder that she hadn't eaten anything at all that morning.

"I think it's the time-space continuum you're experiencing," he explained gently. "Your inner being thinks you're in danger because of the sudden change and is trying to protect you."

She sensed there was more to this story, but he didn't want to scare her further. For now, what she needed most was food and some restorative rest.

"Eat, then rest. Later, we can chat some more," he suggested calmly.

"No! Don't go!" She was filled with fear, but she couldn't quite pinpoint the source of it. She did not know exactly what she was afraid of.

"Don't worry, I will be right here with you," Jahazap told her softly, tenderly stroking her hair to soothe her distressed spirit before retrieving the large tray of food for her. "Now, eat!"

Her favorite coffee brew was steaming on the tray, alongside an assortment of fruits she did not recognize and exquisite pastries of all kinds. Rena eagerly ate with relish, savoring each bite that was both foreign and delicious. Once she was finished, a wave of fatigue washed over her, and she fell asleep soundly with Jahazap gently rubbing her back, feeling safe and protected in his presence.

"THE TREES MAY NOT HAVE EYES LIKE US, BUT THEY'RE SEEING EVERYTHING, EVEN THE DUST."

"THE TREES MAY NOT HAVE EARS LIKE US, BUT THEY'RE LISTENING TO EVERYTHING, EVEN WHEN WE FIGHT AND CUSS."

"THE TREES MAY NOT HAVE MOUTH LIKE US, BUT THEY EAT, SPEAK AND NEVER MAKE FUSS."

"THE TREES MAY NOT HAVE FEET LIKE US, BUT THEY'RE WALKING, EVEN WHILE YOU CATCH THE BUS."

EPILOGUE

Living in the twelfth-dimensional space-time Earth was an experience vastly different from anything she had ever encountered before in her life. Here, the very concept of time flowed in ways she had to painstakingly learn and adapt to, a challenging process that felt overwhelming at times.

It was doing things to her inner being that kept her senses constantly on guard, alert to every shift and change in her environment. Those who knew her and understood what she was capable of felt the weight of that tension as well, also keeping their own guards up in caution. Who would have thought she would become so uncontrollable in this strange new reality? But truly, who wouldn't? Her surroundings were shockingly filled with animals that were supposed to have been long extinct, yet here they were, roaming around freely, putting her on constant edge and forcing her to wrestle with her own rising anxiety.

Miguel, her brother, appeared to be disturbingly comfortable in this extraordinary element, which seemed entirely natural to him. But of course he felt at home—this was where he truly belonged.

Today, he embodied a gigantic mammoth, strolling leisurely along the riverbank with a small herd of similarly sized mammoths, appearing as if they didn't have a single problem in the world. In stark contrast, her soulmate, Jahazap, was careening around in the body of a tyrannosaurus rex.

The day of her arrival in this strange realm was the very first time he manifested himself before her in such an intimidating form, looking ready to pounce at any moment; she had just woken from an exhausting ten-hour sleep, she had fallen into after eating a hearty twelve-dimensional meal. She vividly remembered him gently soothing her, after the strange, loud noise that sent stress coursing through the monster within her upon waking.

When Jahazap burst into the room, she panicked and darted under the grand king-sized bed, screaming in sheer terror. In that moment of fear, her inner monster was beginning to reveal itself when Jahazap's imposing, monstrous head reached under the bed. Upon realizing how frightened she was, he instinctively switched forms, immediately transforming into a more comforting presence to soothe her frayed nerves.

"You can't do that to me. You know how incredibly unstable I am."

"You got that right, honey," he had teased playfully, joining her beneath the bed.

They stayed snuggled there for an enchanting six hours. A smile spread across her lips as she remembered the moment, as if it had just unfolded mere moments ago. The floor had given way, revealing another three-foot drop. They fell into a plush canopy bed, carefully crafted from luxurious fresh green grass that sprouted organically from the ground beneath them.

Above them, a sun was shining brightly, a sun that defied all logic and reason in that peculiar place.

"Why am I gazing up at a sun under the bed?" she wondered aloud, her brow furrowing slightly.

"It's my manifestation, darling; just revel in it," he replied with a playful smirk. The way he had said it, while gazing deeply into her eyes, sent waves of warmth through her. Her racing heart beat wildly, sending waves of anticipation cascading all the way down to her toes. He bent down to kiss her softly but suddenly hesitated, recalling something important.

His eyes scanned the enchanting area where they lay, and to her astonishment, short, dwarf-like fruit trees began erupting from the grassy ground, forming a whimsical gate around them. The ripened fruits hanging from the branches were releasing an eclectic array of intoxicating scents that filled her nostrils, but despite the delicious distractions, her yearning for him was far more desperate than any offered food.

Rena raised her delicate hands and gently stroked his warm, inviting face. She looked deep into his mesmerizing diamond iris eyes and inexplicably found herself falling, helplessly captivated. How was it even possible that she could feel even more for this enchanting soul than the overwhelming affection she was already experiencing? Her eyes had transformed into a blazing flame of vibrant orange, radiating warmth that enveloped him completely, warming him through and through.

"I don't know if I can manage any more of this all-consuming feeling," she confided softly, her voice laced with vulnerability.

"I will help you just as you will help me," he whispered intimately into her ears, moving his mouth tantalizingly close to her lips. Slowly and gently, he captured them in a sweet kiss. Rena felt her body melting like rich, hot butter on a summer day, and she realized his body was also surrendering, melding into hers with an irresistible pull. Together, the two of them melted into one as they seamlessly disappeared into the grassy canopy bed below, like water sinking quietly into the thirsty ground. The fluidity in which they both moved through a twelve-dimensional earth was akin to hot oil, gliding effortlessly at first, then gradually slowing as they flowed through the crevices until they reached another mysterious opening. There, they came to a gentle, languorous halt.

Jahazap was the first to reassemble, standing tall as he stretched out his hands toward her invitingly. Rena felt herself slowly reforming, her essence coalescing. She reached out for his hand, and he pulled her up with tenderness, drawing her back into the vibrant world around them.

"Where are we?"

"Inside twelfth dimensional earth." The space they occupied continued to unfold magnificently with each cautious step they took, revealing a breathtaking and expansive view. Eventually, they arrived at a large, grand granite palace, which was strikingly aesthetically pleasing to the eyes. Rena's gaze fixated on the mesmerizing purple sun, which hung majestically over the palace, leaving her in a state of disbelief. It bathed everything around them in a radiant purple of every hue, delicately mingled with shimmering silver light. It was, without a doubt, the most stunning and surreal scenery Rena had ever encountered in her life.

"Where is the silver coming from?"

"The silver only illuminates when you're around," he explained gently. As if on cue, what appeared to be people began to emerge from the palace, drawn by the enchanting interplay of silver mingling with the vibrant purple. A female figure gradually approached them, stretching out her hands in a welcoming gesture. Rena turned to glance at Jahazap with a raised eyebrow, her curiosity piqued.

"She's your mama in this realm."

"I have another mother?"

"Yes, child. I am your very first soul mother, so don't you ever, for any reason, forget that," the woman said with a gentle yet firm tone that resonated deeply through Rena's very essence.

Rena, overwhelmed by a whirlwind of complex emotions, didn't quite know exactly what to do in that moment. She hesitantly walked up to the ethereal female, her arms outstretched as if drawn by an invisible and powerful thread of destiny.

"It's nice to..." she began to express, but before she could finish her thought, the being that resided within her rushed out to greet the female, recognizing her at once with a profound warmth. In that significant moment, her vessel, which had transformed into a mesmerizing dark shade of purple, eventually collapsed gracefully, but Jahazap caught it tenderly in his strong yet gentle arms before it fell onto the floor. The female held Rena's entire being in her embrace as if it were a delicate newborn, cradling it affectionately against her heart. It curled up blissfully in her arms, a warm and radiant glow enveloping them both.

"My little Assamous, I knew you would return to us," the woman cried, silver tears cascading down her cheeks to land softly atop Rena's being's head, creating a shimmering and unbreakable connection between them. At once, Rena's entire being turned a brilliant silver, and she could no longer hold back her tears of joy and relief. Memories of this woman flooded back to her with vivid clarity, heartfelt emotions stirring within her—the one who had brought her into existence so very long ago and held a sacred place in her heart.

"Maman, I didn't leave you at all. I was desperately coming back, but I got trapped outside the light place and couldn't find my way to you. I met Gerard, and he took wonderful care of me until the earthquake came. I couldn't remember anything after that, not until just this very moment," she confessed.

"Shhh, my little Assamous. You're finally back where you truly belong, surrounded by love and warmth. Your father is going to be so incredibly happy to see you," she reassured, her voice soothing like a soft melody that wrapped around Rena.

"LaPam," Rena suddenly recalled with newfound clarity, her memories igniting the vivid image of the first father of her being, a loving figure she had longed to remember throughout her entire existence.

T R Chambers

ABOUT THE AUTHOR

T R Chambers was born and raised in Kingston, Jamaica. Her journey led her to the United States, where she pursued higher education with determination and focus. She earned an Associate degree in Liberal Arts, along with a certificate in Interior Designing from Monroe Community College in Rochester, New York.

After her time at Monroe Community College, Chambers transferred to the University at Buffalo. There, she excelled academically and obtained a double bachelor's degree in Psychology and Global Gender Studies, graduating magna cum laude. Her educational background reflects a deep commitment to understanding both individual and societal dynamics.

In addition to her academic achievements, Chambers has a passion for traveling. She embraces a nomadic lifestyle, cherishing the diverse experiences and perspectives gained from her journeys. Through her travels, she continues to expand her horizons and deepen her understanding of different cultures.

The Jamaican

NOTE FROM THE AUTHOR

Dear Readers!

I pray you enjoyed reading the first book of The Jamaican trilogy!

Please take a moment to leave a review and visit our website for more info.

www.lazygalswofiyahself-publishingthingsllc.com
www.oldmantreepress.com

ALSO BY TANYA R CHAMBERS

YARDIE AND THE ALIENS

Will Earth survive the attaclaps?

In the quiet, often overlooked corners of Earth, where the ordinary seamlessly blends and intertwines with the extraordinary, three aliens from the distant planet Golealm, located a million miles from our solar system, found that they desperately needed matter to survive. For the first three hundred years, Roboliac, the youngest of the triplets, experienced the world by living in the diverse bodies of many different animals, where each creature taught her valuable lessons about the intricate game of survival. It was only after this extensive period that she shared a vessel with a young shaman in the lush Miombo woodland jungle of Tanzania. During this transformative time, she learned how to adapt and thrive as a human. In the shaman's body, she sired numerous sons, and for over one hundred and fifty years, she resided in Tanzania, always assuming male vessels, until all the offspring she had sired into the world began to spread out far and wide.

Meanwhile, her sister Jalaniac moved to the vibrant Caribbean, specifically Spanish Town, Jamaica, and Laliac, the most secretive of the three, only appear when she felt she was needed.

A full one hundred years into a period marked by the horrors of slavery, Roboliac became inevitably entangled in human affairs when she was tragically forced into bondage. When all the bodies she had sired became obsolete, she survived being sent to her beginning by an explosive inserted in unsavory place. She found herself at Jalaniac house in Spanish Town, Jamaica. There, she was left with Jalaniac, who, unfortunately, was also ensnared in the clutches of slavery and had tragically lost her memory. Roboliac once again sought refuge by living as an animal until her sister finally regained her memory, a moment that sparked joy in her heart, enabling her to happily embrace the role of Jalaniac's daughter and sometimes her granddaughter.

In the year two thousand and twelve, when Roboliac was desperately in need of suitable matter, the chance presented itself through Netty, Jalaniac's daughter who was pregnant and tragically losing the fetus. It was in this moment that Roboliac perceived her opportunity slipping through her fingers, when another extraterrestrial being attempted to seize control of the vital fetus. Had it not been for the timely intervention of her devoted sisters, she would have been irrevocably forced back to her origins.

Unbeknownst to them all, the three extraterrestrial beings who had previously tried to snatch Klam's body without success had cunningly latched onto Netty, transforming her into an abusive mother figure. Norma, being the caring sister that she was, felt compelled to take Netty to see Priscilla, another sister who possessed the extraordinary abilities of a voodoo priestess.

As Roboliac, who had now assumed the identity of Klam, journeyed through this unsettling time, she made a startling discovery: her sister had an incredible power to disintegrate into soil when she was injured, only to later reform herself with resilience. It was during this time that Roboliac uncovers the shocking truth about her human sister, Swofiyah, realizing with dawning terror that she was not human at all, but rather a manifestation of Earth itself come to life in human form. Roboliac became filled with fear as she comprehended the significant implications of this revelation, understanding exactly what that meant for their intertwined fates.

Roboliac shocked her sisters once again when she discovered that she was unable to correspond with them, an unexpected consequence of her merging with the human body named Klam.

In another area of the world, Dan, the powerful King of the Sky Beings, found himself irrevocably in love with a human, Priscilla's daughter, Marshane. Determined to carve out a different destiny for herself, Marshane took the bold step of traveling to China to teach English, seeking a future that diverged sharply from the one she had previously envisioned. The unsettling thought of growing old alone with nine cats, who would inevitably devour her body upon her death, served as the catalyst for her decision to teach English in the Longgang District of Shenzen, China.

Unbeknownst to Marshane, the inner voice she had always relied on for guidance and understanding was none other than Dan himself, the revered king of the sky beings, often known as angels. In a twist of fate, he also happened to be her true love—an embodiment of justice tasked with being the punisher of all evil and vile things that roamed the earth. With a mere opening of his jaws, he possessed the power to make such malevolence simply vanish into thin air.

Meanwhile, it became Dan's solemn duty to gather the sky beings once more now that Earth—known affectionately as Solstilert—was back to face the challenges ahead, requiring every last one of them to join the fight for its survival.

The crucial questions remained: Would Roboliac and her sisters be able to set aside their longstanding differences to offer a helping hand in this dire time? And, crucially, would the humans possess the knowledge and resilience needed to confront the impending attaclapse? Most importantly, with the help of the sky being, would Earth endure this formidable threat that loomed ominously on the horizon?

The Jamaican

OLD MAN TREE PRESS